BEFORE NOW

By the Author

Emily's Art and Soul

Before Now

Visit us at www.boldstrokesbooks.com

BEFORE NOW

by

Joy Argento

2019

BEFORE NOW

ISBN 13: 978-1-63555-525-7

THIS TRADE PAPERBACK ORIGINAL IS PUBLISHED BY
BOLD STROKES BOOKS, INC.
P.O. BOX 249
VALLEY FALLS, NY 12185

FIRST BSB EDITION: SEPTEMBER 2019

CREDITS
EDITOR: LYNDA SANDOVAL AND STACIA SEAMAN
PRODUCTION DESIGN: STACIA SEAMAN
COVER DESIGN BY JOY ARGENTO

Acknowledgments

I sit and write alone. The story comes from me and through me. But once it's formed it needs to be shaped. I am eternally grateful to the people that have helped make this book a reality.

A special thank you to my beta readers. Your kind and generous feedback has made this a much better book.
Tracey Dustin * Julie Spelman * Jackie Tambe
Jennifer King * Jenny Argento * Maryanne Argento
Olessia Butenko * Diane Ronner

Special thanks to my editor, Lynda Sandoval, for helping me figure out this writing thing.

Karin Cole, Ellen Eassa, and Tobie Hewitt, your encouragement, suggestions, and friendship have meant the world to me.

Georgia Beers, thank you for your story suggestions and your gentleness. I have learned a great deal from you, my friend.

Cindy L. McGinley, thank you for the past life regression. It proved to be invaluable, interesting, and more than a little emotional. (Cindy does past life regressions as well as soul retrievals in the Central New York area. Go to her website for more info: www. blackhorseconsulting.com.)

Kate, what can I say? Thank you for the encouragement, for the words you let me steal from you, for everything.

You are at the beginning of the dawn.
Thank you, Dawn.

SCOTLAND, 1466

Searing pain shoots through Isobel's leg as the rock slams into the back of her calf. Her ripped skin leaks blood onto the warm ground. She looks up into the eyes of a madman as he drops the slingshot and charges at her. She ducks and slips under his meaty, outstretched arms, his fingers skimming across her neck, leaving a trail of scratches. The world blurs as she turns and blindly pushes at him with the full weight of her body. He teeters, already off balance from missing his target. His arms flail helplessly, trying to stop his forward momentum. Loose rocks dislodge as his feet slip out from under him and he tumbles over the edge of the cliff. She stares in disbelief as his massive body disappears from sight. Isobel thinks the bloodcurdling scream she hears is coming from her own throat until she turns toward the sound and sees Heather—eyes bulging, mouth wide open.

CHAPTER ONE

The sun was just starting its downward trek on the other side of the lake, the air fresh from the recent rain. Still plenty of time to get the perfect shot. Delany Payton set up her tripod, attached the camera, and made a few adjustments. Streaks of pink and yellow faded into brilliant gold and reflected off the water in slivers of shimmering color. The Universe painted the canvas sky for Delany. Her job now was to capture it.

She enjoyed the solitude photography afforded her. After a long day of teaching, it was nice to have some peace and quiet. Of course, being single for the past several years afforded her plenty of quiet at home, too. But this was a different kind of quiet. The quiet contained within the walls of her house was sometimes lonely. No. Lonely wasn't the right word. She sometimes felt alone, but she wasn't lonely. It felt more like someone was missing who should have been there. She had no idea who she was longing for, or why. She was perfectly content—happy, in fact—being alone. Not that she would have resisted a relationship with the right person. She just wasn't going out of her way to find it.

This evening, nature provided her with plenty of company. An occasional fish leapt out of the water aiming for a bug, coming down with a splash. Birds still flew overhead, not yet ready to settle down for the night. Crickets and frogs sang all around her.

Delany was hoping to get some decent shots that she could take to the Marcus Gallery on Monroe Ave. She wanted to see about the possibility of having her own show there. She needed more photos in her portfolio in order to approach them. If things worked out tonight, she would be one step closer.

She spent the next hour and a half taking pictures, making camera adjustments and framing her shots. She opened the aperture on the camera lens and lowered the shutter speed as the evening progressed into night and the moon took the place the sun had held. It was quite dark by the time she packed up her gear and headed back to her car. The flashlight she'd decided to stick in her back pocket at the last minute definitely made the walk easier than it would have been without it.

Once home, she debated whether to make herself something to eat or to forgo food in favor of uploading her shots to the computer to see what she had captured. She compromised by making herself a chicken salad sandwich and eating it at her computer desk in her makeshift office, otherwise known as the spare bedroom. She took a big bite while she waited for the pictures to transfer from her smart card.

Several of the shots held real promise. She marked them as favorites and moved them to another folder on her computer. She would play around with cropping and color adjustments over the weekend.

Her sandwich finished, she turned her computer off for the night and headed back downstairs with her plate. She needed to get some sleep if she was going to be any use teaching her first class in the morning.

One more hike up the stairs to brush her teeth, wash her face, and crawl into bed and her day would be complete. She was just pulling up the covers when her phone rang. A quick glance at the screen told her it was Abby.

She'd met Abby three years before when Abby had taken one of Delany's writing classes. Abby didn't seem to mind that she was the oldest one in the class, a good thirteen years older than most of the other students, many of whom were fresh out of high school. Abby was writing—or rather *trying* to write—a book on holistic healing practices. She'd ultimately given up the idea, but she and Delany had become close friends in the meantime. Abby was the kind of person you could trust with your deepest, darkest secrets. Not that Delany had any of those, but it was good to know she could tell Abby if she did.

Delany hit the Answer button on her phone.

"Hey," Abby said, before Delany even had a chance to say hello. "Get any good shots tonight? The sunset looked beautiful from my window. I'll bet it was spectacular from the lake."

Delany wasn't sure when Abby found time to breathe. She seemed to talk in a rush at times. "It was great. I got some usable pictures. Surprisingly there wasn't any ice left on the lake." Rochester winters could be brutal, and ice by the shoreline could sometimes last well into May. The warmer weather had started with the actual arrival of spring on the calendar this year, a very unusual occurrence.

"Did you want ice?"

"Either way was fine. Ice would have made for some pretty interesting pictures."

"Speaking of pretty interesting pictures, are we still on for ice cream after work tomorrow? Scoops and Cones in Panorama Plaza opened for the season."

"What does ice cream have to do with interesting photos?" Delany asked.

"Nothing. Although pictures of ice cream would be interesting."

Delany laughed and shook her head. "Sure. What time?"

"I have a client at three. How about we meet around four?"

"That works."

"Great. See ya then. And, hey, get some sleep. You have to be up bright and early for work tomorrow."

"That's what I love about you, Abby. Always looking out for me."

"Of course. I love you, too. Good night."

"'Night."

❖

Jade Taylor stepped out of the shower and toweled herself dry. She'd worked up quite a sweat playing tennis at the health club, but she enjoyed it. It was a good way to expel her pent-up frustrations. Of course, so was sex, but she hadn't had that since she broke up with her partner last year. Hell, she hadn't had sex in well over a year before that. The last part of her relationship with Sheila had been stressful and sexless. It wasn't for lack of trying on her part. Jade had done everything she could think of to try to make things work: flowers, dinners, long talks, time together, time apart. Nothing seemed to work. She realized, after Sheila had moved out, that she didn't even miss her, and all her efforts had been a waste of time.

Nine years of her life wasted. Nine fucking years. She never wanted to repeat that mistake again. No, she was fine alone and happy to stay that way. Well, except for the lack of sex part. Sure, she could take care of her own needs. She was quite handy with a vibrator, and giving herself an orgasm was no problem. But she couldn't kiss herself. Couldn't hold herself at night. Couldn't whisper sweet things in her own ear. She missed that.

Maybe a friends-with-benefits situation was just the thing she needed. No messy, heartbreaking relationship. Occasional sex with someone she liked. What was the harm in that? Granted, she'd never had sex outside of a relationship before, but dammit, she was thirty-four years old. It was time to start doing what she wanted to do. And lately, what she wanted to do was have sex. Enough, she told her brain. All this sex talk without sex action was getting to her. She needed to cool her jets here. She wrapped the towel around her and made her way to her locker.

Nicole, her tennis partner, was slipping her shoes back on, already showered and dressed. The girl didn't seem to sweat, even after the strenuous set they'd just played. Nicole would be a good choice for the friends-with-benefits thing—except for that pesky husband and the fact that she was straight.

Jade smiled to herself and shook her head. This was such a stupid idea and so far removed from anything she'd ever done. Her vibrator would have to do.

"What are you smiling at?" Nicole asked, pulling Jade out of her thoughts.

"Oh, nothing important. Good game today."

"Sure was." Nicole grabbed her purse from the locker. "See you next week." She gave Jade a quick hug and walked away.

Jade watched her exit the locker room, doing her best to keep her eyes off the tight jeans hugging her rear end. *Oh my God. Stop it. You're acting like a teenage boy. You need to figure out a way to get this out of your system.*

❖

"Shit. What the hell was I thinking?" Jade said out loud. *You weren't thinking. You let your hormones get in the way of good sense. You did it now. You actually did it.* She stared at the words on the computer screen. *Email sent.* There was no way to retrieve it. It had already traveled through cyberspace to her friend Abby's computer. *Shit.*

Hopefully she'll think it's a joke. She had never done anything like this before. She wasn't sure why she had done it now. Oh, who was she fooling? She knew exactly why—and that word started with a capital *H* and ended with *orny.*

Even if Abby did take it seriously, Jade doubted she would be able to come up with anyone on such short notice. Her trip to Rochester was only four days away, and she would only be in town for three nights. Not much time for anything—especially what Jade had asked for.

She opened up her Sent Mail folder and reread the note.

Hi Abby,

I'm driving in from Buffalo next week. Hoping we can get together for dinner or drinks. Would love to catch up. Hey, I was thinking, I haven't had sex in over two years. Wondering if you have any single friends I can maybe get together with. Just a thought. Talk to you soon.

Love ya,
Jade

A quick glance at the clock told her it was well past one in the morning. Maybe fatigue was to blame for her lapse in good judgment. She closed the lid on her laptop, rubbed her eyes, and wondered if anything would actually come of this. And if it did, would she actually go through with it? Her libido told her there was a good chance she would.

Chapter Two

A re you trying to pimp me out?" Delany asked.

"No," Abby said, with a laugh. She handed Delany an ice cream cone. "I would have to get paid to be your pimp. No one's offered me any money. Although I do accept tips."

Delany licked a drip of chocolate ice cream from the side of the cone before it reached her hand. "Explain this to me again."

Abby paid the young girl behind the counter, and the two women walked over to a nearby picnic table.

Delany pulled the pictures she had taken at the lake from her backpack and set them on the table before plopping down across from Abby.

"My friend Jade is visiting from Buffalo for a few days. She hasn't had sex in a while and she asked me if I had any single friends. Interested?"

Delany tilted her head toward the warm sun, enjoying the early spring weather while trying to make sense of Abby's words. "Is she looking for a blind date?"

Abby shook her head. "I'm pretty sure she was just asking about sex."

Delany squinted at her friend. How could she agree to have sex with a stranger? True, it had been a long time since she had enjoyed the company of a woman, and the thought of it sent a tingle through her, but sex with someone she didn't even know?

She wasn't sure it was a good idea. "I'd be happy to have coffee with her."

"Delany, she's not looking to have coffee," Abby said. "Look, she's really nice. Beautiful. You'll like her. I've known her forever. Jade Taylor. Look her up on Facebook before you decide. She ended a relationship last year with a total bitch. She's not looking to get into another relationship. I think she's a little lonely and would like to spend intimate time with someone."

"What if I say no?" Delany trusted Abby with her life. She wasn't so sure she wanted to trust her with her *love* life, although in this case, it would be more like her *sex* life.

Abby tucked a strand of short red hair behind her ear. It immediately slipped out and hung across her face again. She shrugged. "Say no if you want. I'm not forcing you. I have other friends I can introduce her to if you don't want to meet her."

A strange panic hit Delany in the gut like a punch. "I didn't say I don't want to meet her." What the hell? She wasn't sure she wanted to do this, and at the same time, she was sure she didn't want Abby to give this chance to someone else. "I'll check her out tonight and let you know."

Abby finished her ice cream cone and grabbed Delany's pictures. "Don't wait too long. No pressure, but she'll be here on Friday."

"Oh, no pressure at all." Delany shook her head. "That's in three days."

"I know. You have three whole days to get ready."

"Ready?"

"You know—shave your legs, buy breath mints, tidy up your bedroom. Trim."

"Ha ha, aren't you just so funny." But Delany hadn't shaved her legs in weeks. No need to when you aren't wearing shorts or a skirt in public, and Delany rarely did that even in the hottest months of the summer, let alone the winter they had just left behind. It was amazing what you let slide when no one was around to see you naked.

"I'm not sure why this is such a big deal," Abby said, turning her attention to the photos in her hand.

"Because, I don't do one-night stands." Delany broke off a piece of her ice cream cone and absently tossed it to a small bird that had landed on the end of the table.

"Oh, I like this one," Abby said, turning the pile of pictures toward Delany to show her what she was talking about.

Delany nodded, more interested in the conversation than the pictures.

"You've done one-night stands. Besides. this would be more like a two-night stand."

"They were never worth the effort. That's why I don't do them anymore."

"Delany, I'm not trying to talk you into this. You can do whatever you're comfortable with. She asked me, and I thought of you. You're close in age. You're kind, funny, and cute. I thought the two of you would hit it off."

"Well, I am cute. And she likes cute?"

"Loves it." Abby smiled. "Think about it. Could be fun."

"Sure, it's all fun and games until someone loses an eye."

"It's just sex. How is someone gonna lose an eye?"

"Oh, I don't know. You get squeezed too hard. Someone loses control of a vibrator. You never know."

"Jade Taylor from Buffalo. Look her up," Abby repeated, and returned her attention to the photos.

Delany threw the last bit of her cone to the bird and let out an exasperated sigh. She would definitely look up Jade Taylor on the computer tonight. What could it hurt?

❖

Whoa, Delany thought as she looked at the profile picture of Jade on Facebook. *She's pretty. Wow.* Jade was beautiful. Her profile picture showed her with a racquet in hand. *Oh, and look, she plays tennis. She's probably super fit. She'll undoubtedly think I'm a slouch.* Delany had played volleyball her first year in college but hadn't played any sport since. As her interest in photography grew, her interest in sports faded. Not enough time in the day for it all.

Delany studied the picture. Perfect features jumped out at her. Brown eyes—light, more like amber—long straight brown hair with a hint of red, a smile that seemed to take over her face, revealing perfect teeth. Perfect. That word seemed to sum up her looks. *No one's perfect.* She must have something major wrong with her. No, Abby would have told her if she was some kind of bizarre freak.

Delany stared into eyes that seemed to stare back through the computer screen. She wondered why Jade had to ask for help to getting laid. *I'll bet she has women lined up waiting to do her.* Delany smiled at herself and her slightly vulgar thoughts. She never talked like that, but sometimes her own thoughts caught her by surprise. *I could so do her.*

She clicked the *About* tab on Jade's profile and read out loud. "Lives in Buffalo. Grew up in Rochester. Oh yep. She plays tennis."

She pulled her cell phone from her pocket and hit Abby's number from her contact list. "Okay. I'll meet her," she said, before Abby had a chance to say hello.

"You slut," Abby said with a laugh. "You'll sleep with the first pretty face that comes along."

"Stop it."

"I'm kidding. I told her you would probably be calling her. I'll text you her number."

"You were that sure I'd say yes?"

"No. But I think you'll like her."

Delany shook her head. What had she just said yes to?

❖

Jade settled down with a glass of wine and the latest copy of *Tennis Magazine*. She kicked off her shoes and pulled her feet up underneath her on the couch. She'd had a rough day at work, and it was good to be able to relax for a little while.

She jumped at the sound of her ringing phone. It was a Rochester number she didn't recognize. Crap. Probably the woman Abby was setting her up with. Abby obviously didn't take the email as a joke. Jade had tried to explain to her that she hadn't been in her right mind when she'd sent the request, but Abby had already told her friend about her, and the friend, Delany, had agreed to meet her. Abby said she was sure they would hit it off. *I can ignore it and not answer*, Jade thought. *This was a really stupid idea.* The ringing continued. What would it hurt to talk to her? She could always say she had changed her mind.

"Hello."

"Um. Hi. Jade?"

"Yes.

"Yeah. Hi. Sorry. This is Delany. Abby gave me your number? I guess I'm a little nervous calling you like this."

Jade doubted that Delany could be any more nervous than she was at that moment. But it was almost cute the way Delany was stumbling over her words. "Nothing to be nervous about. I'm the weirdo who put out that strange SOS," said Jade, trying to reassure herself as much as Delany.

"Yeah, I guess that makes me the weirdo that answered it."

"Well, I'm glad you did." *What? Am I really? Why did I just say that?* Maybe because Delany seemed like a nice enough person. Of course, they hadn't said much more than "hello" so far. But Abby said Delany was great, and Jade trusted Abby's judgment. However, it was her own judgment she was questioning now.

"I hope I'm not calling too late. Abby said you would still be up. So if I woke you, it's all her fault." Delany laughed.

Jade warmed to the sound of it, much to her surprise. "No, I wasn't sleeping. I'm a night owl. Not usually in bed until at least midnight, even though I have to be up early for work."

"Me too." Delany paused. "Abby told me you're in customer service."

Jade wondered if this weird situation was making Delany as uncomfortable as she felt. "Yeah. I lead a very exciting life. I manage that department at the Buffalo gas company." *Look at us talking like normal people. This doesn't seem weird at all.*

"Do you like it?"

Jade tossed the magazine on the table beside her. "It's okay. It's a lot of paperwork, and occasionally I have to field a phone call or two from an irate customer that one of the operators can't handle. I had a customer call me a bitch today because I wouldn't let him pay his bill over the phone." She took another sip of wine. It actually felt kind of nice to be able to share her day.

"Is that unusual? Don't you normally take payments that way?"

"We do. But this guy wanted to pay with cash. Not sure how he planned on stuffing the money through the phone. We get all kinds."

Delany laughed. "I read on Facebook that you play tennis."

Jade wasn't surprised Delany had checked out her online profile. She had done the same.

"I love it. I'm not the best, but I try. Do you play?"

"No. Too much running for me. I usually only run when something dangerous is chasing me or when I shoplift."

Jade smiled. She found herself actually enjoying the conversation. "Do you shoplift often?"

"Not a lot. I teach writing at the community college, and it doesn't pay that well. I only steal to make ends meet. You know—a bottle of wine here, a container of cream cheese there."

"I dream of a world where our teachers make enough money to afford cream cheese," Jade said, playing along.

"I dream of a world where chickens can cross the road

without having their motives questioned. I read that somewhere. I think it was on a T-shirt."

"You're very funny," Jade said. She couldn't help but smile again. "What else do you like to do besides shoplift?"

"Oh, just for the record, I don't enjoy shoplifting. It's actually a lot of work. I write a little. Nothing serious. I think it's mandatory for a writing teacher to write. Oh wait. What's that saying? 'Those who can, do. Those who can't, teach'?"

"Yep, that's it."

"So I'm not sure if that means I can or I can't. But anyway, I try. I'm also into photography, landscapes mostly. I love to take pictures at sunset, when the sky is on fire. In fact, I recently bought myself a new camera."

"You can afford a new camera when you can't afford cream cheese?"

"Hey. Don't judge me. Photography is my passion. Cream cheese is not."

Jade laughed. "I would love to see your photographs sometime." Oops, there it was. She'd just invited herself to see Delany. She cringed. Did she really want to do this?

"Why don't you plan on coming over when you're in town this weekend? I could show them to you."

Jade hesitated. Talking on the phone was one thing, but agreeing to meet in person was another. Going to Delany's house meant she would be agreeing to have sex with her. Wouldn't it? Did her email to Abby mean that it was a done deal? No. That was ridiculous. She could meet Delany in person and still have the option of not sleeping with her. Maybe that's what she would do—meet her, and then decide. There were no rules set in stone here.

"Or not," Delany said, dragging Jade out of her thoughts. Delany must have sensed her hesitation.

"Sure. That would be nice." *There, I said yes. God help me.*

Chapter Three

"These are beautiful pictures," Jade said. She had driven in from Buffalo earlier in the day, spent some time with her parents, and had a drink with Abby before driving to Delany's. She was fine when she left Abby but was hit by a case of nerves as she got closer to Delany's house. After the first phone conversation with Delany she thought maybe this wasn't such a bad idea after all. Or maybe it was. *Who knows? I'm here now. I can always leave if it this gets too weird.* "When you told me you were into photography I had no idea you were this talented. Wow." She wasn't just saying it. The photos on the wall were truly wonderful, something to be admired. Maybe this Delany was, too.

Delany's lips spread into a grin. "I'm glad you like them. If my humor doesn't win the chicks over, I can usually get them with my photographs."

"Well, you have me won over. I'm impressed." Her nerves were still at full alert, but she'd only been here a few minutes. She figured it would take longer than that to feel relaxed. This whole thing seemed a little surreal.

"Hmm. That was easy. I didn't even have to show you my magic lasso or invisible plane." Delany handed Jade a glass of red wine.

"You have an invisible plane?" Jade took a sip. The rich liquid went down easy. Delany had good taste in wine. It would go a long way toward helping her relax.

"Oh yeah. But I can't take you for a ride in it right now. It's got engine trouble, and my mechanic can't seem to see the problem."

"And that would be 'cause it's got an invisible engine, too?"

Delany smiled. "You catch on quick. Come on, let's sit." She led them to an overstuffed couch across from a matching chair. The room was full with furniture, a coffee table, various knickknacks, and personal items, but it wasn't cluttered and everything seemed to fit together effortlessly.

Jade sat and glanced at Delany. If she was as nervous as Jade felt, she didn't show it. Jade studied her features. Her online picture didn't do her justice. Light brown hair framed an oval face. Deep-set green eyes sat under dark brows with equally dark lashes. Abby said she was cute, and she was right. The T-shirt she wore hugged her in all the right places and was neatly tucked into the waistband of her jeans. If Jade had seen her on the street, she certainly would have taken a second look.

"So, Jade, tell me what you do in your free time besides tennis."

"Well." She led a fairly solitary life in Buffalo. It wasn't that she didn't have friends, it was more like she didn't *do* much with them lately. Part of the problem was that most of them were paired off and she was single, and part of the problem was that she was choosy about who she spent her time with. "I like movies, eating out, all the normal stuff. I run—and not because I shoplift."

"Oh sure, I confess one little crime and you throw it up in my face." Delany laughed at her own joke. It brought out the color in her eyes and made cute little crinkles in the corners. "Run? Like in marathons?"

"Oh no. I run to clear my head. Only a mile or two. I try to do it at least a couple times a week."

"And nothing's chasing you?"

Jade laughed. The wine and the easy conversation were definitely easing her nerves. "Nothing's chasing me." She sipped her wine. "Sometimes after work or on weekends, I go hang with my uncle."

"Nice. He lives in Buffalo?"

"Yeah, in a nursing home. Dementia. I'm the only family in the area, so I make sure he's doing okay and has what he needs."

"That must be a blessing for him. How is it for you? Is it hard?"

No one had ever asked her that before. The fact that Delany had warmed her. "It's hard watching him deteriorate. It's both interesting and horrific watching someone literally losing their mind inch by inch." Mostly horrific. "Sometimes he thinks I'm his sister, maybe because I look like my mom, and sometimes he knows exactly who I am. I don't bother correcting him because it only confuses him more. But I love spending time with him. His wife died about five years ago and he didn't have any kids of his own, so I'm the closest thing he's got." Jade never shared most of this information with the people in her life. For some reason she felt comfortable sharing with this total stranger sitting across from her. She wasn't sure why. "What about you? From this area? Is your family here?"

"I have a sister. Our parents abandoned us." Delany chuckled. "They moved to Florida last year when Dad retired."

"You must miss them," Jade said. "I know I miss my parents since I moved to Buffalo, but it's only an hour and a half drive to visit. Florida isn't just a car ride away." She didn't know what she would do without her family, even when her mother was driving her nuts.

"I do miss them, but we talk often. Having my sister here helps. She's married. They have a little girl, Lizzy. She's four. I love that kid. And of course, having Abby in my life keeps me hopping."

"I love Abby." Abby, who'd taken her email seriously and set this whole thing up. She still didn't know whether to thank her or be irritated at her. "She's one of my oldest friends. Speaking of oldest—can I ask you how old you are?" Jade said, changing the subject. "Or is that too personal?" Abby hadn't mentioned it and Jade couldn't quite figure it out. Delany certainly didn't look much older than she was, but on the other hand, she could have been quite a bit younger. She just had that kind of face. A face Jade was finding very attractive at the moment.

"Thirty-six—and age isn't personal. Asking me about—oh, I don't know—my underwear, *that* would be personal. By the way, I'll be thirty-seven in eighteen days."

"What day is that?" Jade asked trying to do the math in her head. "Don't make me count."

"You can either count or we can talk about underwear, which do you prefer?"

Jade didn't answer. She would have to count on her fingers to figure it out and wasn't willing to look foolish in front of this new friend. Friend? Would Delany be a new friend? She certainly felt comfortable with her.

"Underwear? Okay, mine are purple with little pink dots— bikini briefs. And yours?"

"What day?"

"What day do I change my underwear? I try to do it at least twice a week."

Jade laughed. "No. What day is your birthday?"

"Oh, my birthday." Slight dimples formed in her cheeks as she smiled. "April eighteenth. I'm an Aries. What sign are you?"

Jade sipped her wine and felt it warm as it reached her stomach. She was starting to feel a warmth lower as well. It was a familiar feeling, one she hadn't felt in quite some time, but she welcomed it as she would the return of an old friend. She was also surprised by the feeling. It usually took some time to warm up to people, but she felt very at ease with Delany. She was definitely attracted to her.

"Hmm?" Delany raised her eyebrows. "Sign?"

Jade had lost the thread of their conversation. "Oh. Um, Scorpio. But I'm afraid I don't know much about the zodiac."

"Scorpio, huh? That's a water sign. I'm a fire sign. Know what you get when you mix them?"

Jade shook her head.

"Steam." Delany wiggled her eyebrows.

Jade couldn't help but laugh. "Oh, is that right?" The steam was definitely starting to rise inside her.

"So you don't know about zodiac signs. Are you into any metaphysical stuff? Tarot cards? Psychics? Spirits? Anything like that?"

"Not really. I have nothing against it or people that believe it. But I believe this is it." She waved her arm in a sweeping motion. "This is all there is. We live. We die. We're done. So, all of that seems like nonsense to me. But I guess whatever gets you through the day. How about you?" Jade asked.

"Oh, I believe it. Life is like a school that we choose to come to for our souls to learn and progress. We choose the lessons we want this time around and come to earth to learn them."

"I'm not sure why some people would have chosen the experiences they go through. That seems kind of crazy." Jade paused. She hoped Delany didn't think she was calling *her* crazy. "Sometimes things are so hard."

"It's the hard things we learn from. It's when we face our fears and get through the rough times that we grow."

"I never thought about it like that before. I'll have to ponder it. I hope my opinions aren't offending you."

"Not at all. Everyone is on their own journey, and part of your journey is to believe what you believe. But I'll tell you what. If I die before you, when your time comes I'll be the first one to greet you on the other side and say I told you so." Delany's wide smile was infectious, and Jade found herself smiling in return.

"Deal." She offered Delany her hand to shake. When Delany gently gripped it and held it for several beats, the ripple of heat that shot through Jade surprised her. She attempted to hide the feeling with another question. "Did you always have such strong beliefs?"

"I was raised Catholic. Religion class taught all about God and heaven, but for me, it goes so much beyond that. I don't go to church anymore. I consider myself spiritual but not religious."

Jade scrunched her face up in thought and a bit of confusion. "What's the difference?"

"I think of religion as a box. You're taught or *told* what to believe. You're given *their* truths. There are different rules for each religion, although some are very similar. Most are man-made rules."

"What about the Bible? Isn't that filled with rules directly from God? Isn't that what most believers think?" She wasn't being obstinate, she truly wanted to know Delany's thoughts.

Delany smiled. "We could be here for weeks while I explain my thoughts on the Bible. To me, spirituality is everything that is outside the box. It's so much more than any one religion can hold." She paused. "I'm not explaining this very well."

"I'm sorry," Jade said. "I didn't mean to put you on the spot."

"Not at all. Growing up, I pictured the God they talked about in church as this old man sitting on a throne judging us. This is good, that's bad. That sort of thing. I believed in heaven and hell and that what we did directly affected where we would end up after we died."

"And you don't believe that anymore?"

"I still believe in heaven, but I don't believe that God would create us, give us one shot on earth, and then condemn us to hell for all eternity because we screwed up. I believe He loves us too much for that. When my niece was born, it kind of opened my eyes to that."

"In what way?" Not having any siblings, that also eliminated the possibly of nieces or nephews. Jade often wished she had one or two to fuss over.

"I love that little kid. Ya know? I can't imagine anything she could do that would make me condemn her to hell forever. *Because* I love her. I'm sure God loves us even more than that.

In general, I don't use the name God anymore. I prefer to say the Universe. I find it much more encompassing than the image of that old man on the throne."

"Interesting."

"Sorry. I don't mean to be preachy. I'm probably boring you."

"No. Not at all. So why did you stop going to church?" Jade was fascinated by Delany, not only her beliefs but by the woman herself.

Delany shrugged. "I'm not against church. Some people find a great sense of peace and community there. I just don't like it when some of them use God to promote hate. I didn't like the feeling of being locked into their rules."

Jade smiled and raised one eyebrow. "So you're a rule breaker?"

Delany returned the smile. "Oh yeah. I'm a rebel all right." She shook her head. "Not."

So, why had this seeming *good girl* agreed to meet her for the possibility of sex? It certainly piqued Jade's interest.

❖

Delany poured them both another glass of wine, their third. There was something about Jade. Something that felt familiar. Something she was drawn to. But she was beginning to wonder if sleeping together was still an option. They hadn't really talked about it on the phone or in the texts they'd exchanged. As undecided as she had been when Abby first asked her about this, she realized now that she was very interested in seeing the evening end with the two of them in her bed. But Jade hadn't made any moves in that direction. She watched Jade's lips move as she talked. What would it feel like to kiss them? Would they be as soft as they looked? She didn't know what to do. She liked Jade and thought Jade liked her. But she didn't want to offend Jade or put her off if she had changed her mind about this.

"So, tell me more about your photography," Jade said. "Have you been taking—"

"Can I kiss you?" Delany interrupted, surprising even herself. "Because I've wanted to for the past two hours." She waited for Jade's response, never breaking eye contact. A blush rose in Jade's cheeks.

Jade hesitated a moment before answering. "You aren't supposed to ask."

Okay. Does that mean yes or no?

All this time waiting, and Delany still wasn't sure what to do. Silence grew between them as Delany contemplated her choices.

At the moment it got uncomfortable, Jade piped up. "I like that one picture you took of—" Jade's words were cut off as Delany planted a gentle kiss on her lips.

The plan—if it could have been called that—was to kiss Jade softly and pull back to gauge her reaction. Delany didn't have a chance to pull back as Jade's arms circled her and she returned the kiss full force. A small moan escaped from the back of Jade's throat. By the time Delany did pull away, she was finding it hard to catch her breath. She had never been kissed quite so thoroughly before. She actually needed to uncurl her toes. Wow. Just…wow.

Jade stroked Delany's hair and pulled her in for another kiss. A surge of moisture soaked Delany's underwear as Jade's tongue circled her lips and plunged deep into her mouth.

She willed her hands to continue caressing Jade's arms, forbidding them to move to her breasts. Her palms ached with the thought of what it would feel like to have this woman's taut nipples against them. She allowed her fingers to feel their way up to Jade's neck and tangle in her hair, bringing their mouths even tighter together, deepening the kiss.

Oh my God, Delany thought through the haze of passion. *What is it about her?* The realization that she was kissing a stranger struck her. But she didn't feel like a stranger. She felt familiar and warm and…a flash of light behind Delany's eyelids stopped the thought…and the kiss. "What was that?"

"What was what?" Jade asked, her voice ragged.

"That light. Did you see it?" What the hell?

"I didn't see anything. Maybe you were seeing stars." Jade's brown eyes lit up with her smile. "Come here." She pulled Delany's mouth back against hers.

Delany let herself once again be drawn back into the kiss. She saw the light again, but it was warm this time...golden. It seeped from the edges of her closed eyes, into the frame of her vision. A scene played out in her mind.

The light is coming from a fire. A fire in a stone fireplace. She is lying down on a thin, stiff mattress with someone. It's Jade. But it isn't Jade. And at the same time it is. It's them. Young. Different. But them, nonetheless. The image is fuzzy but the feeling is clear. It's love. It flows to her and through her. She can see the person beneath her. Her face. She loves her. Loves her.

"Stop. I'm so sorry. I need to stop." Jade saw the look of disappointment and confusion in Delany's eyes as she came out of some kind of reverie. Green eyes. Beautiful eyes. Jade closed her own eyes to avoid looking at them. She willed her breathing to slow down. Fear mingled with excitement and slowly replaced it altogether. Fear? Fear of what? She blew a lung full of air out in a useless attempt to gain control.

"You okay?"

Jade opened her eyes and nodded. "I'm sorry. I thought this was a good idea, but now I'm thinking maybe it's not. I don't think I'm cut out for the friends-with-benefits kind of thing. I get attached, and I definitely am not in the market for a relationship." She wasn't sure she was making sense.

"It's okay. We don't have to do this."

"It's not that—I mean—it's not that. I don't...Oh, I'm sorry. I don't know what my problem is. It's definitely me, though. It's not you at all. You're great. You're smart. You're funny. You're beautiful. It's me. It's been a while and...well, I guess maybe

I'm not ready. I don't know. I seem to be rambling here. Stop me before I say something stupid." *Damn. What the hell is wrong with me?* Why was she stopping something she had been thoroughly engrossed in a few minutes ago?

"Really. It's okay." Delany tilted her head and looked up at Jade. "But I am going to have to tell Abby that you don't put out." She grinned.

Jade shook her head and couldn't help but smile back. "You are, huh?" She couldn't explain to Delany why she had to stop. She didn't even understand it herself. One minute she was up to her lips in kisses and the next she was in a full-blown panic. Her heart was just beginning to pump out a normal rhythm again.

Delany smiled. It was genuine, and it was beautiful.

I must be crazy to be turning her down. "I know I'm the one who…"

Delany put her finger over Jade's lips. It was all Jade could do not to kiss it. "Shh. Honest. It's okay. Can we at least be friends?" That smile again. "I'd like to be your friend."

"Of course." Jade smiled back. She wasn't sure who started it, but before she knew what was happening, her lips and tongue were joined once again with Delany's. Fire burned inside her and rose to the surface.

Delany pulled back long enough to say, "I thought you wanted to stop."

"Shh…can we just kiss? That's all. Just kiss?" Jade pulled her back in. The fear seemed to have dissipated. It still danced around the corners of her mind, but her body was in control now. She wasn't going to listen to her mind.

"Kissing is good," Delany said, her lips a fraction of an inch from Jade's.

Jade nodded, feeling the heat of having Delany so close. She couldn't believe how well Delany kissed. How well they kissed each other. There always seemed to be a little bit of an adjustment period when she kissed someone new. She had to figure out the right angle to tilt her head or open her mouth to get everything just right. But not with Delany. They meshed together seamlessly.

Her brain had trouble firing thoughts. She was swept up in the kiss and the arms that were around her, pulling her in, feeling full breasts pressed against her own.

Her hand found its way in between them and she cupped Delany's breast through her shirt.

Delany let out a low moan. "Hey. That's more than kissing," she whispered.

"Uh-huh," Jade whispered back. "Is that okay?"

"Mmm."

Taking that as a yes, Jade increased the pressure and felt Delany's nipple harden under her fingers. Fear took a step forward in her gut and she squeezed her eyes tighter against it. She didn't understand where it was coming from. She'd never had this happen before. Of course, she'd never kissed a stranger before. But that wasn't it. It was something about Delany herself. Jade was afraid of being too close to her. Of wanting her too much. *What? Why? Too much thinking*, she told herself and pushed the fear to the back of her mind.

Delany planted small kisses across her face, to her ear, and down to the nape of her neck. Delany undid the top three buttons on Jade's shirt, and the kissing continued down to her cleavage. A tongued dipped between her breasts. A hot shiver traveled through her body, settling squarely in the pit of her stomach before spreading downward. *What is this woman doing to me, and how far can I let it go before I can't stop?*

Chapter Four

"It's up to you. You can tell me if you want. You don't have to. But I know you want to. So, go ahead and tell me what went on last night," Abby said to Delany over the phone.

Delany laughed. Yeah, she was going to tell Abby, and Abby knew it. "Well, not a lot happened."

"What does that mean?"

Delany sat on the edge of the bed, still in her bathrobe, a towel wrapped around her head. She had barely stepped out of the shower when Abby had called for details. "We talked. We drank wine. We kissed…" *Oh man, did we kiss!*

"And?"

"And, I don't know. She stopped me at one point, and then, before I knew it, she was kissing me again." Delany flopped back on her bed. She only had a couple of classes to teach today, and that wasn't for a few hours.

"Um, okay. I mean, was that okay?"

"Yeah. I like her and was definitely interested in more, but she seemed hesitant. Did she tell you any of this? Did you talk to her today?" Delany wasn't sure just how close Jade and Abby were.

"I had breakfast with her this morning. She said she thought you were great, but that's about it. She doesn't share the details of her life with me the way you do. So it never went beyond kissing?"

So she thought I was great. Delany couldn't help but grin.

"Delany?"

"Oh, sorry. There was some touching, too. I didn't want to push it and I let her take the lead, but she led it nowhere. Which is okay. Honestly. I was just sort of confused." Confused might have been an understatement. Delany thought they were really hitting off, and then, out of nowhere, Jade said she had to go. "Around midnight, she said she should be getting back to her parents' house 'cause they were probably waiting up for her."

"Wow. Sorry. Are you still planning to get together tonight?"

"Yeah." Delany was looking forward to it. "We're going out to dinner and then coming back here. I like her, so just being friends would be fine. I mean, I would like more, but..." But it wasn't up to her. "I would like to get to know her better." *Although I sort of feel like I already know her. Like I've known her before.* Delany wasn't sure that would even make sense if she told Abby. She hesitated before continuing. "Something weird happened last night while I was kissing her."

"Weird like how? Like she licked your eyebrow weird?"

"I'm being serious. Weird, like I had a vision or something. I'm not sure how to explain it. We were kissing, and I suddenly felt like I was somewhere else. I was still with her but it wasn't really her. It felt like it was in another time." It sounded even crazier when she said it out loud.

"Like a fantasy?"

"No, more like a memory I was reliving."

"What does that mean?"

Delany struggled for the right words. "Like I was seeing a bit of my life that I had already lived. But it wasn't. Nothing like that has ever happened. It almost felt like I was watching a movie, but I could feel the actual emotions."

"Explain, please."

"In the vision I was kissing Jade, but it didn't look like her. And I didn't look like me, for that matter. I knew it was still us. I know it sounds strange." And it did.

"Are you messing with me?"

"Totally serious."

"That *is* weird. What do you make of it?"

"Not sure what to think. It was probably my imagination taking over." But imagined or not, it had seemed so real. She wondered if it was a one-time thing or…? Or what? She didn't know. She also didn't know if she wanted a repeat of it. The out-of-body experience felt good in the moment, but so did kissing Jade. Jade. She was seeing Jade again tonight. She was looking forward to it and hoping that she had a chance to kiss her again.

❖

Delany wrote *POV* on the whiteboard at the front of the classroom. "Can anyone explain what point of view means?" With a lot of effort, she had pushed thoughts of Jade to the recesses of her mind.

Several hands went up.

"Krista." She pointed to the girl in the back row.

"It's how the story is written, like if it's being told from one person to the reader or like the reader is watching the characters."

"That's part of it," Delany said. "What else can you tell me?" The words echoed back in her head. *What else can you tell me?* But the words were not her own. They were coming from the same girl she saw in the vision she had while kissing Jade the night before. She caught a glimpse of her in her mind, the sun bright on her skin…

Her dress is light brown with white lace trim, her hair golden blond. She's sitting on a large rock, the soft sound of running water close by.

"What else can you tell me?" the vision girl asks again. "What do you like to do when you are not working?"

"My brother says I daydream too often."

"You look like your brother. Same dark hair and dark eyes. Is that what your parents looked like, too?"

"Miss Payton? Is that right?" Her student's voice brought her back to the present. The image was gone from her mind but not forgotten.

Delany realized she hadn't heard any of the girl's answer. *Maybe I should talk to someone about this. Or check in to the psych ward.* What did all this mean and where would it lead?

CHAPTER FIVE

Jade buttoned her blouse, glad she had packed a nice outfit to go out to dinner in. She was looking forward to seeing Delany again—to the possibility of kissing her again. Maybe more. Probably more. She had spent a restless night thinking about the possibilities.

The smell of pot roast cooking wafted up the stairs and into the guest room. Jade's stomach rumbled as she trotted down the steps. She found her mother in the kitchen peeling potatoes at the kitchen sink.

"Smells good, Mom."

"You sure you can't stay for supper, honey?" She rinsed the last potato, placed it in the bowl, and wiped her hands on a green plaid dish towel. Jade recognized it as part of a set that she had given her mother for her birthday a couple of years ago. It was a simple pattern, but Jade had been drawn to it.

"Thanks, but I have plans." Plans she was looking forward to.

"Are you going to be out late again tonight?"

"I'm not sure. Please, don't wait up for me like you did last night." It had been more than ten years since Jade moved out of her parents' home and four since she'd moved to Buffalo, an hour and a half away. But her mother still acted like she was a teenager who needed supervising when she returned for visits. In a way, it was sweet. And in a way, it was annoying.

"Well, you have a key."

"Yep. Thanks. I'll try not to be too late."

"You might want to take a sweater. It's still getting pretty cool in the evenings." A little too much mothering.

"I have one in the car," Jade said. "Love you, Mom." She gave her a kiss on the cheek and headed out the door.

Her thoughts went to Delany. She had asked if they could be friends and Jade wanted that. Looked forward to it, in fact. She liked Delany. There was something very appealing about her. She couldn't quite explain it, but she felt very comfortable with her. Kissing her last night had been great. She'd wanted more, and at the same time something about that scared her—which was pretty damn stupid. She'd been with several women. She wasn't afraid of sex. Afraid wasn't exactly the right word for it. Anxious? Nervous? No, those words didn't seem to fit either. Was it because she didn't really know Delany? She wasn't sure. How could she be so comfortable around someone and, at the same time, freak out with fear when she kissed her for the first time?

She hoped Delany wasn't too disappointed they hadn't progressed much past kissing last night. Jade was actually disappointed in herself and very frustrated by the time she left. Time had flown by last night, and before she knew it, it was midnight. She was torn between staying longer and getting back to her parents' house, knowing they were waiting up for her. Tonight if she was going to take the leap, she had to act on it earlier. She didn't think Delany was going to steer things in that direction after Jade told her that she didn't think sleeping together was a good idea.

How could she be so torn about sleeping with someone? She was driving herself nuts. It wasn't that she didn't find Delany desirable. She certainly was that. "Put it out of your mind," she said out loud. *Oh great. Now I'm talking to myself. Maybe I am going nuts. Well, at least I'm not answering myself.* She signaled to turn into the restaurant parking lot. "Yes, you are." *And you're right. You do need stop thinking about it. Enjoy the evening. Whatever happens, happens.*

A quick look at her watch as she walked in told her she was a couple of minutes early.

"What time is it?" Delany said in a husky voice, directly behind her.

A warm tingle traveled through Jade. She had a sense of déjà vu but dismissed it without much thought.

She couldn't help but smile as she turned and looked at Delany. Her shoulder-length hair had a bit of a curl in it today and she had a hint of makeup on. The warm tones of the peach blouse she wore brought out the brightness of her skin. "It's time for a drink."

"My favorite time of day," Delany replied.

They sat at the dimly lit bar and Delany ordered them both a glass of wine while they waited for their table. The light hum from others talking in the vicinity wasn't overwhelming and Jade relaxed into the soft bar stool. The wine arrived in record time. Jade was far from a wine connoisseur but could identify a good wine with full body richness. It was delicious. She once again silently praised Delany's good taste.

"How did your classes go today?" Jade asked, with true interest.

"Good. I like teaching. When I first started, it scared the hell out of me. I was so nervous. But then I realized no one in the class was trying to kill me, and it was fine." Her eyes lit up with her smile.

That was one of the things Jade liked about Delany, her humor. "That's good. If they were trying to kill you, I would recommend you find another profession."

"You're heading back to Buffalo tomorrow?" Was that a bit of disappointment in her voice?

"Day after that. My parents are having a family dinner

tomorrow, invited some relatives I haven't seen in a while." Jade liked spending time with her family, but spending more time with Delany would have been really nice, too.

"That sounds like fun. I'm donating blood tomorrow."

"Oh, that sounds like fun, too." Jade sipped her wine, enjoying the warmth it caused in her body. Or was being close to Delany causing it?

"I have plenty. Thought it would be nice to share."

"It *is* nice to share. I learned that in kindergarten."

"In kindergarten, I learned that boys are stupid and have cooties."

There was that humor again. Jade smiled. "You must be a fast learner 'cause I didn't learn that until I was in middle school."

"So you didn't date boys in high school?"

"Actually, I did. I had this whole 'trying to fit in' thing going." Jade made air quotes with her fingers. It hadn't taken long for her to figure out that boys were not what she wanted, but girls didn't seem to fit in the idea of what her family and the world wanted for her. "What about you?"

"Didn't date until my senior year. She was in my English class and I fell instantly in love. Of course, no one knew we were dating. Being out at school wasn't an option."

"What happened with her?" Jade turned in her stool toward Delany, waiting for the answer.

"We went to different colleges and just drifted apart. I think we both wanted the freedom to explore other relationships."

"And did you?"

Delany sipped her wine. "Explore? Yeah. Nothing too serious. Longest relationship was a little over two years."

"My longest relationship lasted nine years." Nine wasted years.

"That's a long time to be with someone and have it end. I'm sorry it didn't work out."

"I'm not sorry it didn't work out. I *am* sorry it took me so long to recognize it never should have happened in the first place. It was a long, hard lesson to learn." That was something she never wanted to repeat. Being single was just fine with her.

Delany nodded.

"I was super bitter for a while. I felt like I had been tricked into the relationship."

"How so?"

The bartender set a bowl down in front of the two woman and poured pretzel bites into it. Jade nodded her thanks.

"She was so great at the beginning. Very loving, very giving, very attentive. But it was all an act. She was actually very narcissistic. By the time she started letting her real self slip out into the open, I was so in love that I dismissed it." She had ignored the red flags that had popped up all over the place. "I spent the last half of our relationship trying to get back what I thought we had lost. It took me a long time to understand that we never actually had it in the first place." Jade realized she was revealing more of herself to Delany than she normally did with people. She was surprised to find how easy it was to open up to her.

"Did you have other relationships before that one?" Delany reached for a few pretzels and pushed the bowl closer to Jade.

"I was twenty-four when we met. I had a couple other girlfriends, short term. But she was the first really serious relationship." That one didn't turn out too well. Serious relations weren't worth the trouble and heartache they caused.

The hum around the bar had risen a few decibels as more people crowded around to enjoy happy hour, making casual talking a bit more difficult. Jade was glad when the hostess stepped up to inform them that their table was ready. Drinks in hand, they followed her and sat down. The dining area was much more comfortable on all levels. The small light that hung above their table gave off just enough light to easily read the menu, but not so much it was glaring. The glow illuminated Delany's bright eyes. Jade had a bit of trouble keeping herself from staring into them. She purposefully concentrated on the menu in her hand. After a few long beats, the easy conversation continued.

Jade had a slight buzz from the wine by the time they finished eating. She wasn't sure she should drive.

Delany seemed to read her mind. "How about I drive us back to my place, if you're still up for coming over? We can come back and get your car later."

"Sounds like a plan." She did want to go back to Delany's place. And she did want to sleep with her. But she still wasn't sure if she should.

Jade was quiet on the ride back as she tried to sort through her feelings.

"Doing okay?" Delany covered Jade's hand with her own.

The jolt of electricity it sent through her was surprising. "Yep." Jade smiled to reassure her. She felt like she needed to reassure herself as well.

Back at the house, Jade excused herself to go to the bathroom. She splashed cold water on her face, looked at herself in the mirror, and shook her head. "Make up your damn mind," she whispered.

"Hi," Delany said, when she came out.

"Hi yourself."

"What would you like to drink? Coffee, water, more wine maybe?"

"Water would be great." Coffee would keep her from sleeping tonight and more wine was simply a bad idea. She made her way to the living room and once again studied the photographs on the wall.

Delany returned a few minutes later and set two glasses of water down on the coffee table.

Jade, without hesitation or any real thinking, put her arms around Delany, pulled her in close, and kissed her full on the mouth.

Jade's body reacted as soon as her lips touched Delany's.

Wow. *What is this woman doing to me?* The electricity that surged through her landed squarely in her center. She wanted nothing more than to take Delany by the hand, pull her upstairs to bed, and make love to her. It was almost too much to bear. This was the moment of truth. She laced her fingers through Delany's and brought Delany's hand up to her mouth. She looked into Delany's eyes as she kissed each of her fingers, one by one. Yes, she wanted this woman. Wanted her now. She pulled her in for another kiss. A deep kiss. A wondrous kiss. A kiss filled with promise of what could be. If Jade could let it be. If Jade could only… But she couldn't. Something stopped her. She wasn't sure if the extreme heat running through her was from excitement or pure panic. Both feelings coursed through her in rapid succession. She stepped back and took a deep breath.

The look on Delany's face was questioning.

"Let's, um…can we sit down?"

"Sure." Delany led them over to the couch. "Drink some water. You look pale all of a sudden."

Jade took a few sips and tried to gather her thoughts. But she couldn't make sense of them. She liked Delany. Found her attractive and was very drawn to her. But… *But what?* She didn't have an answer for her mixed feelings. She knew she must be making Delany crazy with this, coming on to her one second, pulling back the next. It might be best to call it a night and leave. But that was stupid. She wanted to spend time with Delany, not go running off with her tail between her legs like a scared puppy.

"I think I need to leave," Jade blurted out. She saw the confusion in Delany's eyes but couldn't offer her a reasonable explanation. How could she, when she didn't even understand it herself?

❖

Delany struggled to keep the disappointment in her heart from reaching her face. "Do you have to?"

"I do. I'm sorry."

"Any chance of seeing you tomorrow?" She raised her eyebrows, waiting for the answer. Anticipating a no, but hoping for a yes.

"I wish I could. But I can't. I have that family thing."

Damn it. "Oh yeah." She didn't want to push, but she truly wanted to see Jade again.

"I've enjoyed spending time with you and, well…kissing you." A blush rose in Jade's cheeks.

"Me too," Delany said. "Can we stay in touch when you go back home?"

"Of course."

Jade's answer sounded so positive, but Delany had her doubts.

"I'd better be on my way." She wrapped her arms around Delany and hugged her.

"You might want to wait so I can give you a ride back to your car. Did you forget you left it at the restaurant?" At least there would be a little more time with her.

"Oh my God, I did. How stupid."

The time went by too quickly, and Delany found herself parked next to Jade's car before she knew it. "Well, I guess this is it," she said, certain it was the last time she would see Jade. Maybe that was for the best. Jade seemed to pull back each time they got too close.

"I guess so." Jade leaned over and kissed her quickly on the lips. Then kissed her again and let it linger. The third kiss was much more involved and quickly deepened. The small moan that escaped from Jade's throat sent a surge through Delany. *I really hope I see her again.*

"I feel like a teenager making out in the car," Jade said, with a smile. She kissed Delany one more time and opened the car door. "I really did have a nice time."

"Me too."

"Good night," she said quietly, and got out, closing the door behind her.

Delany watched as she got into her car and drove away with a wave.

Damn, Delany thought. *Damn. Damn. Damn.*

Her cell phone rang as she pulled into her driveway. It was Abby. Of course.

She answered without saying hello. "How do you know I'm alone and not in the middle of some hot girl-on-girl action?"

"'Cause, I just got a text from Jade saying she was heading back to her parents' house and that she had a good time with you. So, I'm calling to ask you what kind of a good time she had."

"Oh my God. Can't a girl have a little privacy here?" She turned the car off and slipped the key in her coat pocket, but made no move to get out of the car.

"Sure. If you want to keep it private, you can. No problem."

"All right, stop begging. I'll tell you." Delany proceeded to give Abby a recap of their evening.

"Sorry it didn't work out the way you wanted it to. I'm not sure why Jade changed her mind."

"It's okay. I'm glad I got a chance to spend time with her. I like her."

"Any more visions while you were with her?"

"Actually I had one this afternoon while teaching. Freaked me out a little. It seemed so real. When I was with Jade tonight—I don't know, there was such a feeling of familiarity." It confused Delany as much as it brought her comfort.

"You know, I was thinking about what you told me. I talked to my friend Valerie about it. She's the medium that has the office next to mine. She does past-life regressions. She thinks it could be a memory from a past life." The Downtown Healing Center, where Abby's office was, housed various types of natural healing and metaphysical services.

Delany let the idea roll around in her head before answering.

"I don't think so. It was so clear. I mean, you know I believe in past lives, but I've never heard of anyone actually remembering them."

"She and I have talked about it before. All kinds of crazy things can happen. I think you should make an appointment to see her and either have a psychic reading or a past-life regression. What do you think?"

"I don't know. It probably doesn't mean anything. Although I have to tell you that I really, really like Jade. These are pretty strong feelings I seem to be developing all of a sudden." Might be better to just drop it all and forget it ever happened. These feelings would probably lead to nothing but heartbreak if she pursued it. Jade had made it clear she didn't want a relationship, and Delany believed she meant it.

"You said you felt like you'd known her before. Maybe you have—in a different life. It would be interesting to see if maybe you did. Have you told Jade any of this?"

"No. She doesn't believe in an afterlife. I don't think she's going to believe in a *past* life. I don't want her to think I'm crazy."

"She spent the last two evenings with you. I'm sure by now she knows you're crazy."

"True, but I don't want her to think I'm insane."

"I'll text you Valerie's number as soon as we hang up. You decide what you want to do, but I think you should call her."

Delany got out of her car and said she'd consider it but doubted she would follow through. She didn't bother with the lights once inside. She took off her jacket, kicked off her shoes, and plopped down in the armchair. Tired but restless, she flipped on the TV. She drifted off to sleep somewhere in the middle of a *Cagney & Lacey* rerun.

She's standing on the edge of a cliff. At her feet, pebbles fall over the brink and tumble far below. She takes a step back and looks around. Patches of small violet flowers blanket lush, rolling green hills. In her hand is a bouquet of the same purple flowers. She pulls out a stem and gazes at the clusters of small bell-shaped blossoms. Suddenly the wind picks up and sweeps the flowers away. As if in slow motion she reaches for them. Her fingers graze the edges as they tumble away, down the cliff and out of sight. A green plaid blanket lying on the ground nearby, also caught by the wind, flutters away and follows the flowers down into the abyss. A bird circling overhead shrieks at her and flies away. She watches until it becomes nothing more than a dot in the sky.

Delany woke with a start, the dream still vivid and alive in her mind. She made her way to the bedroom, undressed, and crawled into bed. She couldn't shut her brain off as the dream mingled with the two previous visions she'd had. Trying to sort them out and make sense of them was no use. Any attempt she made to reason them away was also useless. There had to be an explanation for them. She just wasn't sure what it was. Maybe it was time to find out.

CHAPTER SIX

Delany's foot tapped out a steady rhythm as she thumbed through an old copy of *People* magazine in the waiting room. Nothing to be nervous about, she reminded herself. Maybe she *was* going crazy and should be seeing a counselor or psychiatrist instead of a medium.

"Delany?"

She heard her name and looked up.

"Sorry to keep you waiting. I'm Valerie." The older woman took a step forward. The gray hair pulled into a ponytail and the thin knit shawl around her shoulders gave her the appearance of being older and somehow wiser. "Come on back, and we'll get started."

"Great," Delany answered, feeling less enthusiastic than she sounded. She followed Valerie past a few closed doors to a small, brightly lit room. Several framed nature prints hung on the dull green walls. Most had uplifting messages or words.

Gratitude.

Trust that the Universe knows what it's doing.

Open the door to miracles.

A well-padded office chair was pushed up to a small desk in the corner, and a brown recliner sat against one wall. Patchouli and sandalwood incense permeated the air. It somehow seemed to calm Delany's nerves. She supposed that was the purpose.

Valerie pulled a set of blinds down, making the room considerably darker. "Have a seat and make yourself comfortable. Ever had a past-life regression before?"

Delany sat and shook her head. "You do this through hypnosis?"

"Yes. It's basically a relaxation technique. Not like you see on TV where people cluck like chickens. That's not real." Fine creases etched around her eyes with her smile. Delany guessed her to be in her early fifties.

Delany leaned forward in the chair. "Is it possible—if I give you a name, can we try to find out about a past life I may have had with her?"

Valerie pulled out the office chair, sat down, and pulled a yellow legal pad and pen out of the top desk drawer. "We can go with the intention of finding that person in another life. There's no guarantee, though."

"Her name is Jade Taylor. Do you need to know more than that?" Delany drummed her fingers nervously on the arm of the chair.

"No." Valerie scribbled a note on the pad. "Now, when you're under—well, I say under, but you're aware of everything at all times. Hypnosis is a collaborative effort between the client and the practitioner. So, if you're fighting me, you're fighting against yourself. Some people decide they are going to resist it, almost like they want to prove me wrong."

"Oh no. I honestly want to see if we can find something out."

"Okay. Good. Make yourself comfortable. Sit back. Put your feet up if you're all right with that."

Delany did as she was told. She lifted the handle on the side of the chair and raised the footrest. She clasped her hands together.

"We need to get you relaxed," Valerie whispered. "Do you have any other questions?"

Delany shook her head and took a deep breath. *Okay. Here we go.*

"I want you to know that we're going to create a safe place for you in case any of this gets too intense."

The visions she'd had so far had been intense. Delany wondered if this would feel the same.

Valerie continued. "It can be a real place you've been to, or someplace you make up in your head. Let's decide where that is now. Have you done anything like that in meditation?"

"I have," Delany said. "I find sitting by the ocean very peaceful, so I usually picture that." She crossed her legs at the ankles, uncrossed them, and then crossed them again. She absolutely needed to relax if this was going to work. She hoped Valerie could make that happen.

"Good. If you find at any time that you are feeling agitated or upset, or if I see you are, I may ask you if you want to go to your safe place. If you feel that way and I don't ask, you can raise one finger as a sign to me. It can become an auto signal. Sometimes our bodies and subconscious mind know better what we need than we do."

"Okay." Another deep breath.

"Any fears that I should know about? Anything? Like bridges?"

Delany only gave it a moment's thought. "No. Nothing."

"Great. Lean back. Close your eyes. And uncross those ankles."

Delany rubbed the back of her neck and followed the instructions.

Valerie talked her through some breathing exercises, taking her deeper into a relaxed state with each breath. Her voice seemed to get a little farther away as Delany pictured the images Valerie described. The nerves seem to seep out of her pores and were replaced by peace.

"As you drift along in this natural state, so deep, so relaxed, you see a cloud. Imagine being on this cloud. Soft and comfortable. As you sink into it, allow everything else to flow out and away. Breathing and relaxing."

She continued on and Delany felt like she was moving far from here.

"Filling your heart with a white light, keeping you safe and…"

Delany's eyes seemed to roll higher in her head as the words drifted around her.

"You see a man guarding a bridge. This bridge will take us to the past. To a life you've lived before. He asks for your password to cross. The password is your name. Tell him. He is our guide. You're here to explore. Perhaps you're here to find Jade from another life…"

Delany found herself crossing the bridge in her mind and stepping back firmly onto the earth—an earth that was somehow different. Greener. Pure. Untainted.

"Take a moment to look around you. Hear, see, smell, taste, touch all that is around you. Do you know where you are?"

"Scotland." Delany heard herself answer but didn't know how she knew that.

"What year is it?"

"Fourteen sixty-five."

"Look down at your feet. What do you see?"

Delany's own voice seemed distant as she answered. "Nothing."

"You're barefoot?"

"Uh-huh."

"What are you wearing?"

"A white dress. No. It's more like a tunic, tied at the waist. It's simple, dull, white. Covered in the front by an apron. The apron is thick, like canvas." In her mind, Delany reached down and touched the material. It was coarse, well-worn, almost soft from age and wear.

"What else do you see? Describe it."

Delany looked around. There were people everywhere. Young, old, heavy, thin—and horses. It was loud. Men shouted. Others talked and laughed. In front of her was a wooden cart with two large spoked wheels on one end, two legs and a handle on the other. Brightly colored vegetables filled the top of the cart. People passed by carrying things—loaves of bread, fish, baskets of eggs. A marketplace. *It's a marketplace.*

Valerie's voice, from somewhere far away, asked her what her name was.

Delany tried to think, to remember.

"Isobel. What are you daydreaming about this time?" she hears a voice say. It's her brother, Tomas. She turns toward him. He's taller than she is with a head full of curly, dark brown hair. His face is smooth, not the face of a boy, but not the face of a full-grown man either. His shirt is the same shade of dull white as the clothing she wears. His brown wool pants are held up by a belt made of rope.

"Isobel?" Valerie said, from somewhere else.

Delany realized she'd told Valerie the name Tomas had called her.

"How old are you, Isobel?" Valerie asked.

"I'm seventeen."

Tomas hands her—Isobel—several yellow squashes that she places neatly on the cart in front of her. Two children with bright red hair run past, squealing with delight, one chasing the other.

The sun feels warm on her skin. She closes her eyes and turns her face toward it. The sound of laughter makes her turn her head and open her eyes. A girl about her own age stands about twenty feet away. But they aren't called feet, Delany's—Isobel's—mind says. What are they called? She lowers her head to think. What is the distance called? An ell? Is it an ell? Is she about thirteen or fourteen ells away? Does that even make sense?

She looks up at the girl again. The flutter she feels in her stomach—or is it her heart?—surprises her as the girl returns her gaze, a slight smile on her lips. The girl is whispering something to the large man standing beside her. Isobel can't see the color of her eyes at this distance but she can tell they're bright with a sparkle about them. A light. Her hair hangs straight down, well past her shoulders, the color of pure honey. Her blue dress is much fancier than the smock Isobel wears.

"You most certainly shall not," the large man says, loud enough for Isobel to hear. He wraps his massive hand around the girl's arm and gently drags her off. She keeps her head turned and her eyes firmly on Isobel as he pulls her along. She stumbles.

Isobel reaches out as if trying to stop her from falling. But the hand gripping the girl's arm keeps her upright until she can get her feet underneath her again. The man shakes his head. The crimped dark hair shakes with it. He is obviously losing patience with her.

A smile breaks across Isobel's face. That is the most beautiful girl she has ever seen.

Valerie's voice creeps in. "What's the girl's name?"

"I don't know. She didn't tell me her name. We didn't speak."

"All right. It's time now to move to another major event. Let's move to a significant time earlier in your life. One, two, three. Where are you now?"

Delany's mind fought to keep the image of the girl in her head as she was transported further back in time. But the girl faded away as something else came into view. "I'm in some type of a house. A cabin. I'm not sure what kind of a house it is. It seems to be only one room. The furniture is bulky. Thick. Made of wood. A table with benches. The room is kind of dark. There are two lit candles on the table, but most of the light in the room is coming from the stone fireplace." Stone fireplace. There was a stone fireplace. The same fireplace Delany had seen behind her closed eyes when she first kissed Jade. The bed. She looked around the room and spotted the bed. The same bed she and Jade lay on in her mind's eye. She pictured the scene again. Yes, this was the place she saw. A tear ran down her cheek. She wasn't sure if it belonged to her or to Isobel.

The girl she had lain with in front of the fire was the same girl she had seen at the marketplace. *She was the girl I was kissing here, in this very room.*

"Bellie?" It's her brother, but he's a young boy now. "Bellie? Isobellie. We have to go with Uncle Ray."

"Why?" Isobel asks, her voice so little and pure. She looks up at her older brother.

"Because Mum and Da had an accident."

"But why? When are they coming back?" She addresses the question to Tomas but looks toward her uncle by the door. He doesn't smile. She doesn't think he ever smiles.

"Bellie, they aren't coming back. They died."

Isobel isn't sure what that means. They have to come back. They always come back.

Tomas starts to cry.

"Now, now," the uncle says, "we'll have none of that."

Tomas wipes the back of his hand across his eyes and puts his arm around Isobel. "Come on, Isobel. We have to go now. It will be fine. I promise to take care of you. We have to go live with Uncle Ray." He leads her to the door. Uncle Ray steps back to let them pass out into the dark night, lit only by a full moon. He closes the door behind them as the two young children's lives change forever.

Warm tears ran down her cheeks. She shifted in her seat.

"Do you need to go to the safe place?" Valerie asked from some distance away.

Delany didn't want to leave where she was. She didn't want to leave the cabin and the place Isobel knew as home. But she had to, just as Isobel had to.

Valerie repeated the question. She sounded a little closer this time.

"No," Delany answered.

"How old were you when your parents died?"

"I'm four. Only four."

"Do you go and live with your uncle?"

"Yes. And Tomas."

"Did your uncle have a wife?"

"No."

"Did he treat you well?"

Delany shook her head. "No. But Tomas took care of me. He looked out for me. My uncle tried. But he didn't know what to do with children."

"Tomas was good to you? Were you close to him growing up?"

"Yes. He made sure I had what I needed. He was my savior."

Valerie's voice faded into the background again, a dance at the edge of Delany's mind. "Is there anything else you would you'd like to tell me about this before we move on?"

Delany shook her head.

"At the count of three, move forward into the next significant event or time in this life. One…two…three. What's happening? Where are you now?"

"I'm in the marketplace again and I'm talking to that girl. Her name is Heather. She's told me her name is Heather."

Heather's blue eyes light up with her smile. A slight dusting of freckles skims across her cheeks. "Who is the older boy you work with here?" she asks Isobel. The vegetable cart separates them as the late-afternoon sun moves across the sky. The crowd has thinned from the morning rush.

"'Tis my brother, Tomas. And the man in your company?"

"My brother." Heather wears a dress similar to the one she was wearing the first time Isobel saw her. It looks finely tailored and soft to the touch, a pale shade of brown. Isobel pulls at the hem of her own dress. It's the same one she was wearing that day. It's the only one she wears to work. It's the only one she owns.

Isobel waits for a couple strolling by to pass before she speaks again. "He looks like a full-grown man."

"He is. He is much older than I. He believes he owns me. My mum died last year and he has taken it upon himself to tell me what to do and how to live. I detest it."

"Where is your father?"

"Off to war years ago, never to return. We have no word of him. My brother is all I have left."

"My parents died when I was but a wee lass. I have barely a memory of them. My uncle took us in."

"That is horrid."

Isobel shrugs. She has long ago accepted her fate in life.

"Shall we meet at the stream in the woods behind MacGregor's tower th'morra?" Heather touches her sleeve.

Isobel looks down where Heather's hand rests on her arm. Before she has a chance to sort out the confusing feelings it causes, Heather's brother is there taking Heather by the arm. His eyes burn a look at Isobel. "Off with you." He pulls Heather along with him as he marches away.

Heather turns and mouths the words, "Meet me tomorrow morn," to Isobel.

Isobel feels heat rush up from her chest to her face. She breaks into a smile.

"What makes you so happy this day?" Tomas asks, returning with a basket of beans.

"Life," Isobel answers. "'Tis life."

"So, you feel happy right now?" It was Valerie asking. Her voice seemed out of place.

"Yes," Delany answered. Or was it Isobel answering?

"Who in *this* life—in Delany's life—is Heather? Is she in this life in the form of another person?"

Delany pictured Heather in her mind and watched her slowly morph into Jade. Heather and Jade were the same person. The same soul.

"Jade. She's Jade." A warmth rushed through Delany, filling her with emotions she couldn't identify. The intensity caused more tears to flow.

"We are going to let the past go now," Valerie said. "When you're ready, you can let the veil drop slowly over that life and that part of you." She talked Delany across the bridge of time and back into the present.

Delany took the tissues Valerie offered her and wiped her soaked face.

There it was. Delany *did* know Jade in another life. No wonder she had such a strong attraction to her now. She wanted—no—needed to see her again in this life. The question was, did Jade want to see her? If not, how could Delany change her mind without scaring her away?

CHAPTER SEVEN

Warm water ran down Delany's back as she lost all track of time. She had just stepped into the shower when a scene played out before her—inside her.

Isobel rises with the sun and dresses quickly. She grabs a small loaf of bread and slips out the door quietly, so as not to wake Tomas or her uncle. Half running and half skipping, she heads to the stream behind the tower. Having no idea what hour Heather wants to meet, she is taking no chances. She'll wait all morning for her if she has to. Sitting on the largest rock by the water, she feels the warm breeze on her skin and breaks off pieces of bread to eat. She wishes she had thought to bring a crock of honey.

"So what happened?" Abby asked. "Did you find anything out?"

Delany unwrapped her burger, lifted the top bun, removed the pickle, and set it down on a napkin. "It was interesting. Intense. I went back to a life where I was, I don't know, like a working-class girl, very poor." The food court was quiet. Meeting after the lunch rush hour had been a good idea.

"Was Jade there?"

"She was, and obviously a higher class than me."

"Did she look like she does now? How did you know it was her?" Abby took a massive bite of her burger and stuffed two fries in her mouth before chewing.

"She looked different. I just sort of knew. It's hard to explain. I was still me—who I am now, and I was aware of that. But at the same time, I was Isobel and felt everything she felt."

"You going to tell Jade any of this?"

"She would think I'm insane." Delany shook her head. "There's no way I can explain this to her. Did she say anything about me?" She looked into Abby's eyes, waiting for an answer and not sure she wanted to hear it.

"I get the feeling she likes you, but she's told me repeatedly that she doesn't want a relationship. Not sure what to tell you. You barely know her, really. How you can have such strong feelings for her?" Abby ripped the paper off her straw and stabbed it through the plastic lid on her cup of soda.

"I know it's crazy. But it's like I *do* know her. Like I know her soul. Her essence. I remember her. Getting to know her in this lifetime is just a formality." She held up her hand, stopping Abby from responding. "As I said, I know it's crazy. I just feel if she gave it a chance…if she gave me a chance, and we spent time together, she would feel it, too."

"What are you going to do?"

"I don't know. I should just drive to Buffalo, rip her clothes off, and make love to her until she screams. That might help her remember."

"I'm thinking the screaming would start as soon as you ripped her clothes off."

"Okay, probably not the best idea. But I'm so unbelievably frustrated. Any suggestions?"

"This kind of puts me in a peculiar spot. You're my friend and I want you to be happy. But she's my friend, too, and I have to respect her wishes. If she doesn't want to date you, there isn't anything I can do about it. The original request was for someone to have sex with, nothing more."

"I know. I didn't expect to feel this way or have these—these"—she held her hands up and searched for the right words—"memories, or whatever you want to call them." She shook her head. Even she had trouble understanding it. How could she expect anyone else to?

"Are you planning on doing another past-life regression to see if you can find out more?"

"I don't think I need to. I'm starting to remember stuff on my own. It's like a private little movie running through my head. It's so real. The thoughts. The feelings." The feelings. Delany was surprised by the intensity of them. "Like I'm living it now."

"But you aren't living it now. This is a whole different life, and even if you had a past life with her, that doesn't necessarily mean you should be having *this* life with her. You might want to take a step back and try to figure out if these feelings you have for her now are real or if they are leftover feelings from another time."

"I know. I feel so...I don't know, connected to her." Delany finished her fries and helped herself to one of Abby's. "Do you think I should get my head examined?"

"I think you should get your heart examined. That's what seems to be so tied up here."

"Any suggestions on how I go about doing that?"

"I wish I had the answer for you. I don't."

Delany didn't either. But she was determined to find out. She just hoped she didn't push Jade out of her life forever.

❖

Delany wasn't quite asleep when the movie reel running through her head started.

A flock of wigeon ducks swims by and Isobel tosses them a handful of bread bits. They quickly scoop them up and beg for more.

"Sorry. 'Tis all for now. I need to share with Heather," she tells them. Heather. She's waiting for Heather. Her heart rate quickens at the thought, and she smiles.

The morning air has a bit of a chill, but the unusually sunny day is rapidly warming it. Even the strong winds seem to be cooperating with the promise of the day, offering no more than a gentle breeze. It seems like hours pass before she hears a noise behind her and her name spoken out loud.

"Isobel?"

She turns and watches Heather walk toward her. Her dress is simpler today, light brown with lace trim. It is still much nicer than Isobel's. But the dress pales in comparison to her smile.

"Hello," Isobel answers, suddenly shy. "I brought us something to eat." She holds out the half-eaten loaf of bread.

"How sweet," Heather says. "I had the very same thought." She hands a woven basket across to Isobel. "Go ahead. Look."

Isobel lifts the soft cloth covering the contents and peers inside. Fresh bread, meat jelly, honey, and apples. "This puts my loaf of bread to shame," she says, her inadequacy causing the heat to rise to her face.

"Not at all," Heather replies. "We shall add it in and feast later." She sets the basket aside. Pulling up the hem of her dress, she sits on the rock beside Isobel. "'Tis a beautiful day. Is it not?"

"Beautiful," Isobel responds, her eyes never leaving Heather.

"Tell me about you, Isobel."

"What would you like to know?"

"Whatever it is you wish to share. I know scarce little about you. I wish to know much more."

Isobel knows her life will sound boring, the life of a peasant, compared to the rich life Heather must have. "'Tis not much to tell, I fear. My life is simple. My brother grows what we sell and I do the cooking and cleaning for the men, of course."

"Oh, but there must be so much more to you than that. What

else can you tell me? What do you like to do when you are not working?"

"My brother says I daydream a lot." Isobel shrugs. There isn't much more to tell. She absently picks at the tall grass.

"You look like your brother. Same dark hair and dark eyes. Is that what your parents looked like, too?"

She shrugs. "I do not remember them much." The pain Isobel felt as a child with the loss of her parents has faded to a dull ache. Her memories are few. She doesn't find it hard talking about them. She just doesn't have much she can share. Questions posed to her uncle were usually met with disdain. "No need to know such things," he would say. Tomas doesn't remember much more than she does.

"Such a shame, it is. Daydreaming is good. I do so often myself."

"Why does your brother drag you away when you talk to me?"

"Irving does not understand about friends. He wants me only to be with people the same as us. He means well."

Isobel lowers her eyes and picks at a loose thread on her smock. She is not the same as them. She is so much less.

"He is wrong," Heather says, taking Isobel's hand. "I do not think the way he does."

This does much to help Isobel feel better.

"Come." She stands, pulling Isobel up with her. "Let us go swimming." She runs to the stream, tugging Isobel behind her.

At the water's edge, Heather removes her dress and shoes, leaving her chemise on. She wades out into the hip-deep water. "Come on," she says and splashes water toward Isobel.

Isobel hesitates. Her undergarments are patched and stitched together from years of wear. Slowly she removes her shoes and looks over at Heather. The smile on Heather's face tells her all is well, and she strips off the smock.

Heather reaches out her hand to Isobel as Isobel wades toward her. At the last second, Heather retracts her arm and sends a cascade of water at Isobel, thoroughly soaking her. Heather throws back her head and lets out a roar of a laugh.

Isobel stands stock-still for a moment, then lunges at Heather, pulling her down into the babbling water. Isobel once again finds her footing and stands up. Heather takes a few seconds longer to follow suit.

It's evident from the frown on Heather's face and knit brow that she isn't pleased with Isobel's antics. Isobel is about to apologize when Heather's face breaks into a grin and she laughs again. Isobel joins in. This is going to be a good day indeed. She so looks forward to spending it with Heather. There is a promise in the air.

Chapter Eight

Jade put the last of her clothes in the laundry and her suitcase on the shelf in the hall closet. She'd put it off since she returned home from Rochester, but it was done now. Her cat Cliché was curled up on her desk, and she moved him out of the way so she could open her laptop. He meowed his protest.

"I know. I leave you here by yourself for a few days and you think you own the place. Next time maybe I'll have you stay at a boarding kennel instead of having a pet sitter come by to check on you."

In his usual nonchalant way, he jumped down, sashayed across the room, and jumped up on the bed.

Jade watched him go, then turned back to her computer. She wanted to send Delany an email. She just wasn't sure what to say. She had been unable to get her off her mind since they had spent time together and, well, all the kissing. The kissing. The wonderful kissing. She pushed the thought and surge of electricity that came with it out of her mind. Maybe going for a run later, to put it out of her body as well, would be a good idea.

Delany had called her a couple of times, but Jade hadn't picked up. She sent Delany a quick text on Sunday, saying "busy with family," and left it at that. She wasn't sure why. Maybe it was because she really *did* want to talk to Delany that she had avoided it. A relationship was the last thing she wanted, especially long distance. Okay, an hour and a half wasn't that far away. Oh, it didn't matter how close or far apart they were, they weren't going to be starting anything. She wasn't really sure what Delany wanted anyway, but she figured she should put an end to any possible relationship ideas before they even got started.

She typed. She deleted. She typed again. Finally, she had an email that said what she wanted to say—but not exactly what she was feeling. Something about Delany intrigued her—drew her in and scared her at the same time.

Kissing Delany was great. She wasn't sure why she hadn't let it progress further. She wanted to. She did. She knew Delany had been disappointed. She had never meant to hurt her. Being with Delany made her feel something she hadn't felt in a long time. Alive. Sexy. Wanted. That was the reason she couldn't get Delany out of her head. Maybe that was the reason she had changed her mind about sleeping with her. This was exactly the thing she was afraid would happen. Jade had wanted to touch her, to kiss her, to taste her, to…to what? What more was there than that? She had asked for sex. And she wanted sex, wanted to be with Delany. But…

She was making herself crazy with all these thoughts. None of it made any sense. She pushed them from her mind and reread the email she had just written.

> *Hi Delany,*
>
> *First, let me say I had a very nice time and I'm glad I got the opportunity to get to know you a little. I'm hoping we can be friends but want to be very clear that's all we can be. I told you I'm not looking for a relationship and can't handle friends-with-benefits, and that's still true. I just wanted to let you know where I stand. So if we're on the same page with this, great. Hope to hear back from you.*
>
> *Jade*

It sounded cold and impersonal. They had been anything but impersonal several days ago. Making it sound friendlier might give the wrong impression. Jade read it one more time and hit the Send button.

"There it goes," she said to Cliché.

He didn't answer.

"I hope she doesn't think I'm a jerk."

He let out a loud meow.

"Oh, to that, you have something to say? That better mean 'of course she won't think you're a jerk. You're a super sweet, wonderful, caring person. Why would anyone in their right mind think you're a jerk?'" She stood and scooped the cat up in her arms. "Come on, big fella. I better feed you before you change your mind and think I'm a jerk after all. And then I'm going for a very long run." *I have to get this out of my system. I hope I can.*

❖

"What a jerk," Delany said. "I know the rules. I wasn't pushing." Heat rushed to her face and she clenched her jaw.

"If you know the rules and all she did was reiterate them, why is she a jerk?" Abby asked, pulling her small car into the mall parking lot.

"I don't know. She isn't. I am. I guess I liked her more than I should have."

"There aren't rules about how much or how little you're allowed to like her. Feelings are feelings. They aren't right or wrong." The women made their way across the parking lot, disrupting the garbage gulls feeding on any scraps they could find.

"They're wrong if only one of us is having them."

"That doesn't make any sense." Abby held the large glass door open for Delany. "I thought you wanted to be friends. Isn't that what she was saying?"

Abby made sense, but instead of making Delany feel better, it somehow pissed her off more.

"Yeah, in a roundabout 'don't fall in love or lust with me' kind of way."

"And what's the problem with that?"

"I think I'm already falling in a tiny bit of love and/or lust with her." Her attempts to push it down didn't seem to be working.

"I'm sorry I ever introduced the two of you," Abby said.

Shit. That wasn't the reaction she wanted. She just needed to vent. "Don't say that. I'm not. If what it was is all it will ever be, then that's fine. I don't regret it and I *know* she doesn't want more."

"But you do?"

Delany shrugged and considered how much more to confess to. "I'd be lying if I said I haven't thought about it. I know I barely know her. I know. I know. I know. I don't know. I don't know what it is about her."

Abby stopped and sat down on the wooden bench in front of the fountain inside the main entrance. She looked up at her friend. "Are you sure you aren't mixing up the past-life stuff with the current-life stuff? Are you falling for her or are you falling for Heather?"

Delany sat down next to her. "Can't I fall for both?"

"Oh, honey, Heather doesn't exist. At least not anymore. And the one who does—Jade—doesn't want a relationship. I'm sure it's not personal against you."

"How could it be? I'm great. Right? Awesome, in fact?" Delany laid her head on Abby's shoulder, defeated.

Abby put her arm around Delany. "Awesome for sure, honey. Great and awesome."

Maybe Jade just needed to see how great and awesome she was. Maybe there was a way to show her.

❖

Delany sat down at her computer, opened Photoshop, and imported one of the photos she'd taken of the sunset at the lake. She adjusted the contrast and compared it to the original shot. The pinks and yellows blended together as her eyes lost focus and her awareness went to the movie reel that played out in her mind.

Spending time with Heather makes Isobel's heart sing. They are meeting again this very day. She skips out of the house, latching the door behind her, in search of Tomas. She finds him in the field. He looks up at her, runs a tan hand through the curls on his head, and wipes the sweat from his brow. "I suppose you are off to spend time with your new friend again, leaving me to toil alone." A touch of a smile dances at the corner of his lips.

"I would hardly call her new. I have known her for weeks now. Tomas, please do not mind if I go for a wee bit. I shan't be long. I will surely help with the harvest when I return." Isobel says a silent prayer that he won't object.

He waves his hand at her. "Off with you, lass. A girl's place should not be in the fields all day. It is nice to see you have some fun."

Isobel can't contain her smile as she runs off in the direction of the stream.

Heather is already there, lying on her back in the grass under the shade of a large oak tree. One arm drapes over her eyes, keeping out the bright noonday sun directly overhead.

Isobel sees her and slows her step, careful to avoid snapping twigs and alerting Heather to her approach. She silently eases herself down on the ground next to Heather and for several seconds just watches her, taking in the smooth skin, full red lips, the tiny cleft in her chin. She leans over, her lips inches from Heather's ear. "What time is it?" she whispers. "I think it's time for fun, not for sleep."

Heather springs up to a sitting position, hand to her heart.

"You 'bout scared me to death." She laughs. "You realize I must take my revenge on you for frightening me so?"

Isobel settles herself beside Heather. "Oh, you do, do you? What kind of revenge do you think might do? Should I be scared?"

"Oh, it will be wretched, all right. Maybe a frog down your dress or some other horrid deed. One never knows."

Isobel smiles at the thought of Heather chasing her through the meadow, frog in hand, waving it at her.

"Do not smile at me, girl. I mean what I say." But Heather's smile matches Isobel's.

"Sorry for the fright." Isobel does her best to stifle her giggle, without much success.

"Yes. I can tell by the way you laugh how sorry you are."

Heather stands and offers her hand to Isobel, pulling her to her feet. "Come on. Let us go for a walk." She links her arm through Isobel's.

Isobel's heart warms and threatens to burst from her chest with happiness.

Jade filled in the sign-out sheet and slid the clipboard across the desk to the receptionist.

"I sent Steve up to get him. They should be here any second, Jade."

"Thanks, Pam." Jade crossed the small lobby of the nursing home and sat in one of the upholstered, always uncomfortable chairs to wait for her uncle. She didn't have to wait long. She rose to greet him as he came into view.

"Hey, Uncle Willy," Jade said. She kissed him on the cheek. It wasn't that long ago that she had to stand on her tiptoes to reach him, but time and age had reduced his height and given him a permanent stoop. She exchanged greetings with the young man who had retrieved him, led her uncle back to the sitting area, and sat down across from him.

"How are you today, Uncle?"

"Fine. So fine. Do I know you?" He wiped at his chin with a thin finger.

"I'm your niece. Jade. I've come to spend some time with you. Is that okay?"

His wide smile showed several gaps where teeth used to be. "Of course. Jade. Now I remember. I'm glad to see you. It's been years."

She didn't bother telling him that she'd been here to visit three days ago. "You doing good, Uncle Willy?"

"I am. I am. They have the nicest people here at this place. Why, only this morning someone asked me if I wanted a glass of orange juice. It doesn't get any nicer than that."

"I'm glad. I thought we could go out to dinner if you're up to it."

He reached into his pocket and pulled out a few dollar bills. "Here," he said, shoving them toward Jade. "Take this and take someone in your family out to dinner."

She smiled and shook her head. "I want to take you out. You *are* my family."

"I can't go. I have to work." He continued to hold the money out to her.

"Won't they give you some time off for dinner?" Jade knew with dementia you have to meet them where they are. It would do no good to tell him he had retired years ago.

"Let's walk." He stood and plunged the money back into his pocket. "The walls have ears."

Jade had to hurry to catch up to him. She knew better than to let him out of her sight.

"So I was saying..." He pushed open the front door and squinted up at the sky. "What was it I was saying?"

A warm breeze greeted them, along with several robins searching for food in the spring grass. "I asked you about going out to dinner. But we can talk while we take a nice walk around the grounds."

"Dinner, huh? I can't go to dinner. I have to work. I work at the bank, you know. Banker's hours."

"If you have banker's hours then you got off work an hour ago. So, you're free for dinner." The scenario was different, but the struggle was familiar. "We can go to the Copper Pot, around the corner. You've always liked that one."

"Hey, let's go to dinner, you and me. What do you say, Millie?" he asked, calling her by her mother's name.

"You don't have to work after all?"

"Oh hell. I can call in sick once in a while. I haven't done that in years. They take me for granted there." He shook his head. "It's such a shame. I give them the best years of my life and they can't even give me one day off."

Jade took her uncle's arm and gently turned him around. "Come on. Let's go this way so we can go to eat."

"Eat? Didn't I already eat today?"

❖

"I need to take my leave soon," Heather says. "Irving will be expecting me."

"Where did you tell him you are?"

They lie shoulder to shoulder in the tall green grass picking out shapes in the clouds floating by. This spot by the creek has become their favorite place to meet. The peacefulness and the company of Heather fills Isobel's heart.

"For a walk."

"'Tis an awfully long walk. You have been here for hours."

"Did I stay too long?"

Isobel rolls onto her side and watches Heather's face. "Not for me. You never stay too long." She longed to spend even more time together. "I wish Irving would leave us be and not carry on so about us being friends."

Heather runs her fingertips up and down Isobel's arm,

sending goose bumps across her flesh. The tremor that travels through Isobel surprises her. She has never felt such a thing before. She likes it.

"Me too. I like being with you, Isobel. You are very special to me," Heather says. "You know that, do you not?"

"That I am special?" The truth of it makes Isobel's heart beat faster.

"Yes. That you are very special." She leans up on her elbows.

Isobel can feel Heather's warm breath near her face. It makes her own breath catch in her throat. She leans in, closer to the warmth, and closes her eyes. She is not surprised when she feels Heather's lips on hers. She has wanted this, has dreamed of this since the first time she saw her. She knows she should be afraid but is not. This feels more right than anything she has ever done. The kiss is over almost as soon as it starts, and Isobel opens her eyes.

Heather has a look of anticipation on her face, like she is afraid of what Isobel's reaction to the kiss will be. Her reaction is to kiss Heather again. She lets the kiss linger and feels a strange stirring in her nether regions. Tingling. Pulsing. Warm.

"You are very special to me as well, Heather," Isobel says, her voice barely above a whisper.

Heather sits up. "I should be going."

"Are you leaving because I kissed you?" Isobel sits up as well. She holds her breath, waiting for the answer.

"No, silly girl. I liked that you kissed me. Besides, I kissed you first."

"Would you kiss me again?"

"I do not know. I have heard that too much kissing in a day can make a girl go absolutely blind." She smiles.

"You did not. Surely you made that up."

"Maybe I did and maybe I did not, but we cannot take any chances now. How will I be able to see how beautiful you are if I go blind?"

"I am far from beautiful." Isobel looks down at her frayed smock.

"Oh, but you are." Heather gently lifts Isobel's chin and softly kisses her again. "I cannot help but kiss you. Blindness or not, I will take my chances. Besides, I did make that up."

Isobel tickles her sides. The sound of Isobel's laughter mixes with Heather's until they are out of breath and collapse on the ground, Isobel on top of Heather. She gazes down into Heather's eyes, feels Heather's hands in her hair. Heather pulls Isobel's head down to her and kisses her, slowly at first, then with more urgency. Heather's tongue slips between her lips and Isobel hungrily welcomes it in. She is so lost in the feeling of Heather that she barely hears a voice in the distance. They pause, lips still pressed together. The voice comes again. "Heeeather," it calls. It's Irving.

Isobel's eyes open wide as panic sets in. She starts to get up, but Heather's arms around her stop her from moving and Heather rolls her over onto her back. Heather plants one last kiss on her lips, rises, and without a word runs off in the direction of her brother's voice.

Isobel lies on the ground, her breath heavy in her chest. She rests her arm across her eyes and smiles. She has kissed Heather today and Heather has kissed her. Her smile widens until she is sure her face can't contain it.

"Fare thee well, my love," she says.

Delany smiled at what she had just experienced. That was what these memories had become—experiences for Delany. A past life she got to revisit. She pulled herself into this life and immediately thought of Jade. She wasn't sure when all this started if she was separating Jade and Heather in her heart. She knew now she was. Her feelings for Heather belonged to Isobel. Her feelings for Jade—and she had to admit to herself that she did have feelings—belonged to her. *Crazy. I barely know her.*

Maybe it was just physical. They had spent more time kissing than talking. She wanted to spend time getting to know Jade. She didn't know if that was going to be possible. But she had decided she needed to try.

CHAPTER NINE

"Hey, Squirt," Delany said, scooping her niece up in her arms. "Oh my, Lizzy, you're getting big."

"Aunt Delany, am I getting too big for you to hold?" The question came with a giggle.

"Never. I'll still pick you up and hug you when you're fifty."

"That's silly."

"You're silly."

Mary, Delany's sister, came out of the kitchen wiping her hands on a dish towel. "Hey there. How's life in the fast lane?" She was two years older and two inches taller than Delany. She'd inherited their mother's pale complexion and light blond hair, while Delany took after their father with her brown hair and dark brows.

Lizzy was the spitting image of her mother. Delany put her down and gave her a gentle swat on the butt as she ran off. "I'm hanging in there." She gave her sister a hug.

"What's wrong?"

Delany laughed. Her sister always did have a way of reading her mind. "Who said anything was wrong?"

"I know you. Come into the kitchen and talk to me while I finish getting dinner ready." Mary led the way with Delany close behind.

Delany grabbed a couple of raw baby carrots from a bowl on the counter before plopping down in a chair at the table.

"Speak." Mary stood at the kitchen island ripping lettuce into a salad bowl.

"Nothing to speak about really. I met someone."

Mary stopped ripping. "When? Why am I only hearing about this now? You don't sound happy about it. Who is she?"

"Wow. Can you fit any more questions into one breath?" She shook her head. "It's complicated." That was certainly an understatement.

"It always is."

Delany ignored the good-natured dig. "No. *Weird* complicated. Promise me you'll keep an open mind when I tell you this." Getting her sister's take might be a good idea. The only other person she had talked to was Abby, and Abby was too close to both her and Jade to be levelheaded. Oh, let's face it. Abby wasn't always levelheaded on a good day.

Mary pushed the salad bowl aside, obviously ready to give Delany her full attention.

"I mean it. Promise me. 'Cause this is very strange, even for me."

"Okay, I promise. Tell me what's going on."

Delany told Mary about Jade, the visions and the past-life regression. She left out the part about meeting Jade for the purpose of having sex. Mary interrupted her a few times with questions but, for the most part, listened intently.

"So," Delany said, when she finished. "What do you think?" She trusted her sister to be gentle. She hoped she would also be honest. Maybe.

"I'm not sure what to think. Past-life stuff is more your thing than mine. I still go to a Catholic church, for God's sake. No pun intended. You're the one that has gone crazy with all this New Age stuff. The only one we're supposed to believe was reincarnated was Jesus."

"You jerk. That was resurrected, not reincarnated."

"Oh. See how much I know?"

"Do you think I'm crazy?"

"No. Of course not. I just don't very know much about this. I mean, I believe you, of course. It's hard for me to wrap my head around." Mary went back to her salad fixings as they continued to chat.

"I know. Me too, actually. I'm learning more about that life all the time. It's like real memories that are coming to me. Like I'm being shown a movie that's in 4-D."

"4-D?"

"It's like 3-D, but with emotions. I can actually feel what Isobel feels. Most of it feels good. But I felt the confusion and fear when my—I mean, Isobel's parents died. I don't know how else to explain it."

"So, are you going to see Jade again?"

There was the sixty-four thousand dollar question. "I want to, even if it's only as friends. I would really like to have her in my life."

Lizzy came barreling into the room and climbed up on Delany's lap. "Aunt Delany, will you read me a story?"

Delany smoothed the blond hair down on her head and kissed the top of it. "In a few minutes, honey. Let me finish talking to Mommy first."

"Okay." She ran out of the room as quickly as she had run in.

Mary added chunks of tomatoes to the lettuce. "You should call her again. What do you have to lose?"

Well, I could lose her altogether. "I don't want to scare her off."

"I'm wondering if she's already running scared."

"What do you mean?"

Mary paused. But before she had a chance to answer, Lizzy came running in with an armful of books, doing her best to balance them but spilling some on the way. She set them on the empty chair next to Delany and ran back to pick up the ones she had dropped.

"Which one do you want to read first?" she asked, her little cheeks flushed with excitement.

"Lizzy—" Mary started.

Delany interrupted her. "It's okay. We can finish this later. It looks like I have more than a few books I need to read."

Lizzy turned toward her mother. "Is it okay, Mommy?"

Mary nodded. "Sure. Aunt Delany and I can finish later. Daddy will be home for supper soon, anyway."

"Yep," Delany said, and picked up *The Cat in the Hat*.

"We *will* finish this later," Mary said to her sister.

Yes. They would finish it later. Delany hoped Mary could help her figure out the direction to go with Jade.

❖

"Dinner was awesome as always, Sis." Delany patted her stomach. "I'll help you with the dishes."

"I'll help, too," Lizzy exclaimed.

"How about you get ready for bed?" Mary said. She looked at her husband. "Honey, can you help her? I want to talk to Delany for a bit."

"Sure, babe." Kevin got up. "Come on, monkey, let's get your jammies on."

Lizzy looked at Delany with disappointment on her little face.

"It's okay, squirt. You get ready for bed. I'll come tuck you in before I go."

This seemed to appease the child, and she went running off with her father close behind.

Delany piled the plates and carried the stack into the kitchen. "What were we talking about before?" Delany asked. "Oh yeah. That I'm crazy because I'm having past-life memories and falling in love with a woman who has been dead for centuries, as well as falling in love with her reincarnated soul in another body."

"Yep. I think that about covers it." Mary filled the sink with hot water, adding a squirt of dishwashing liquid.

"You were saying something about Jade running scared. What did you mean by that?" Delany asked.

"If you're feeling this, maybe she is, too. And, if she doesn't want a relationship, then these feelings would be scary to her." Mary loaded the sink with silverware and glasses.

Delany took in her sister's words, letting them bounce around in her head before answering. "I don't know what's going on with her. She seemed to like me when we were together, but now..." Delany grimaced. She grabbed a dish towel and set about drying the glasses as Mary set them in the dish drain. "That email seemed...I don't know. Kind of cold."

"I think you should give her another chance." Mary examined a fork in her hand and gave it another scrub with the dish cloth. "You say you'd be okay being friends, right?"

Delany nodded.

"Call her. Be her friend."

"Right," Delany murmured, focusing just a bit too hard on drying the glass in her hand. "Okay. I can do that."

"Can you?"

Delaney scoffed. "Of course."

But the words felt forced.

She wasn't sure she was being entirely honest with Mary... or with herself.

❖

Delany sat at her desk after her last class of the day and pulled her cell phone from her pocket. She pressed the number for Jade and leaned back in her chair. *This is the last time I'm reaching out*, she thought, not sure whether that was true or not. She was about to hang up, sure it was going to voicemail, when Jade answered, breathless.

"Hello."

"Hi, Jade, it's me, Delany." *Wow, witty line.*

"Oh hi, Delany. I didn't recognize the number."

Disappointment punched at Delany as she realized Jade didn't have her number programmed into her contacts list. Maybe Jade didn't even consider her a friend.

Delany swallowed, momentarily at a loss for words. She fiddled with a pen on her desk.

"Still there?" Jade asked.

"Still here. Um, I was wondering how you're doing?"

"Great. And you?"

"Glad to hear it. I'm doing fine."

"Good. Good."

Next line is mine. It was so easy to talk to her before. *Guess she only wanted to get laid, and since she changed her mind about that, she has no interest in me. Or maybe she changed her mind because she has no interest in me.* "Anything interesting happen at work lately?" Delany could hear the sound of rustling paper through the phone.

"No. Listen, I just walked in with an armful of groceries. Can I put these away and call you back later?"

"Oh sure. No problem." Delany tried to keep her voice light and hide her disappointment. She was sure she wouldn't be hearing from Jade again. Frustrated, she hung up the phone.

Jade hit the End button on her cell phone and stared at it, her heart racing. Her cool demeanor with Delany was hard to pull off. Trying to sound aloof when you really want to talk to someone wasn't easy. But it wasn't fair of her to lead Delany on. She suspected Delany wanted more from her than mere friendship, and that wasn't going to happen. If she *was* looking for a relationship, though, Delany would be at the top of her list.

She pulled a carton of milk from the paper grocery bag and put it in the refrigerator. She nearly tripped over Cliché when she turned around. "Hey there. No, you aren't getting any milk. That's a myth. Milk really isn't good for you."

Cliché stared up at her.

"Would I lie to you?" she asked him. "Never. I don't lie. Lying only causes bad things to happen." Of course, sometimes the truth did, too.

She scooped him up, walked to the living room with him in her arms, and sat down on the couch.

"It's probably better not to tell anyone anything anyway. *You* never tell your secrets." She scruffed up the fur on his neck. "You're a lot like me when it comes to that. No good could ever come of it."

Cliché jumped off her lap and strolled away.

"Yeah. I don't blame you. I wouldn't want to be around me either." She went upstairs and changed into shorts, a sports bra, and a T-shirt. She laced up her running shoes and jogged down the stairs, grabbed the house key from the counter, and headed out the door.

Jade power-walked to the nearby park and started a slow jog around the track. The pace picked up with the pace of her thoughts until she was in an all-out sprint. But no matter how fast she ran, she couldn't outrun herself.

❖

"Are you sure we'll be alone?" Heather asks.

"Yes. Tomas is working in the field all day and my uncle never comes here." Isobel pulls up the latch and swings the heavy door open. She steps back to let Heather pass into the home she lived in before her parents died.

Isobel comes here sometimes to be alone and think and sometimes to try to remember. The furniture is as it was when she was a child. On occasion, she runs a damp rag over everything to keep it clean. She washes the spread on the bed in the creek nearby and hangs it to dry on the line. She has been especially particular in her cleaning lately, hoping Heather would agree to spend time with her here.

Heather had agreed immediately.

Isobel lifts the thick wooden plank holding the shutters closed and opens them, letting in both fresh air and rays of golden sunlight.

"Would you care to sit?" she asks Heather, patting the thick, worn bench. Isobel sits next to her.

As if they are of one mind, they reach to each other in the same instant and clasp hands.

"Are you sorry we kissed?" Heather asks.

"Oh no," Isobel answers. Delighted would be more accurate. "Are you?" She holds her breath, waiting for the answer.

"No. I would like to kiss you again. I told my friend Maura that I kissed you. Please do not be angry with me."

"What?" Isobel's eyes widen as panic nicks at her heart.

"No need for worry. She will not tell. She made a promise never to let the truth be known to anyone. I trust her."

Isobel swallows hard. She's not sure about this. She doesn't know Maura. She hopes Heather's correct and her friend is trustworthy. Heather's brother must never find out that she and Heather spend time together. That they kiss each other. Never.

"She will not, I tell you. I know who I can trust."

Isobel rises and paces around the room. The panic expands and lodges in her stomach. Heather stands and gathers her in her arms. "No one else knows. No one else will ever know." She kisses her on the forehead, the cheek, the lips.

Isobel can't help but respond. Her body is commanded by Heather's kiss. She presses tighter into Heather's arms, feeling her own breasts push against Heather's. Her nipples strain against the cloth of her undergarment, longing to be touched.

She knows not of a man's love, but only that of this girl, this woman standing before her. For she does love her and feels love in return. Heat rises from her very center and threatens to burn her with desire.

She pulls back. "Wait. I must slow down, for it is too much."

"I know," Heather says. "For me as well." She takes Isobel's hand in both of hers and holds it to her chest. "My heart beats for you so. I do believe it has waited for you the entirety of my life."

Delany sat up in bed and put her hand to her own pounding chest. She sighed, not sure what to do with these feelings. Isobel's feelings.

CHAPTER TEN

No, everything's fine," Jade said to Abby, via Skype on the computer. "Why do you ask?"

"Checking in on you. I haven't heard from you much since you went home."

"You know what they say, no news is good news." Jade ran a hand through her hair. She had been feeling a little self-conscious around Abby since her request for a lover and even more so after not following through with it. Jade didn't have many close friends, didn't feel like she needed them. But she considered Abby to be special, someone she could trust no matter what. Jade wasn't sure why she didn't trust many people. She just didn't.

"You used to do that when we were kids whenever something was bothering you."

Jade looked at Abby through the computer screen. "Do what?"

"That thing you just did with your hair. If something's bothering you and you want to talk, I'm here for you."

Jade wasn't about to make a full confession about having feelings for Delany. Shit, she barely knew Delany. None of this made sense.

Abby and Delany were close, and Jade figured that either Abby would tell Delany or Abby would feel bad keeping it a secret from her. Either way, it wasn't good. Besides, Jade didn't tell her problems to other people, not even Abby. Of course she told them to Cliché, but he wasn't like other people, being a cat and all. And when he wasn't being uppity, he was a good listener. As if on cue, the cat jumped up onto her lap. She gently scooted him off.

"I do that when I'm tired." She did do it when she was tired. Okay, she also did it when something was bothering her, but she wasn't going to admit that.

"How come you're so tired?" Abby asked.

"Too much work, not enough play, I guess." Jade rolled her eyes.

"I saw that. Okay. I'll drop it. I just wanted to make sure you were all right. So if you say you are, then you are."

"Thank you. Tell me how you are. I'm sorry we didn't get to spend more time together while I was there."

Jade wasn't sorry about the time she'd spent with Delany. In the end, she wasn't sorry she had sent that request to Abby either, even if she had changed her mind about following through. The feelings Delany stirred in her were surprising, and she wasn't quite sure what to do about them. *Nothing.* There was nothing to do about them. She would put them where she put so many of her other feelings. She would bury them somewhere deep inside her. Her feelings never got her what she wanted in life anyway, so why bother with them?

"Are you even listening to me?" Abby's words interrupted her thoughts.

"What? Sorry."

"Where'd you go there? I know you weren't with me."

Jade blinked. "I don't know. Lost in my own head for a minute. Sorry. What were you saying?"

"I asked if you had any plans in the near future to come back here."

Jade smiled. "Miss me already?"

"In fact, I do. And I know Delany would like to see you again."

The smile faded. Jade shook her head. "Nope." Best to stay away from there for a while. Stay away from Delany. Stay away from any possibilities. Jade let her mind wander to the possibilities.

❖

Heather looks beautiful in her red broadcloth dress with the fancy lace trim and velvety nap. Isobel can't help but notice the way the material makes the swell of her full breasts look. Full and inviting. She longs to touch her. To kiss her. To even just talk to her. But it isn't allowed. She's here at the party to work, not celebrate the birthday of the one she loves.

She's sure Irving had no idea she would also be serving at the party when he hired Tomas to cater it. Or maybe he did and maybe that's why he chose Tomas, so that Heather would see her as someone beneath her: a servant, nothing more.

Isobel watches Heather from across the room, sneaking glances when she can. Irving stands at her side, his hand on her shoulder. His unruly hair has been tamed for the occasion, his rough beard trimmed.

Heather looks her way and smiles. Her eyes light up as if from within and Isobel reads her love there. A slight tilt of her head tells Isobel all is well and she is thinking of her.

Irving catches Isobel's look and takes Heather by the elbow, leading her across the room, turning her back to Isobel. They are quickly joined by a troop of young men eager for Heather's attention. She is well into the marrying age, and many wish for such a union with her.

Any jealousy Isobel feels is displaced by her knowledge that Heather is hers, and hers alone. She lowers her head and smiles to herself.

"What is that grin for?" Tomas asks, coming up beside her. He looks across at Heather, then back at his sister. "Remember

we are here to work. Do not get yourself into any trouble. We need our day's pay." His words hold no rancor, only kindness.

Isobel nods. She pours wine from the earthen carafe into goblets and sets them on a tray, which Tomas brings to the large table in the center of the room.

Heather sashays over to Isobel, an empty goblet in her hand.

"More wine, m'lady?" Isobel asks.

"More kisses," Heather whispers.

Heat rises from Isobel's chest to her face. "Where is your brother? I cannot believe he has let you out of his sight." She pours wine into the goblet.

"Outside talking to a nobleman. He wants to talk of marriage with him."

"He wants to marry a nobleman?" Isobel says with a laugh until the realization dawns on her that he's talking of marrying Heather to the nobleman. Her last meal threatens to come up at the thought.

"I will refuse. He cannot make me marry and move away."

"Away?" Isobel asks, acidic panic rising to her throat. She is sure she will vomit with this news. "Away where?"

"I do not know. He rode a fortnight to get here. Fear not. I will not go. I refuse to be married."

"Can he make you? What say do you have in this?"

"There will be no betrothal. Mark my words. I best be getting back to my guests. I just wanted to bid hello to you. I will see you tomorrow, will I not?"

"Yes. Tomorrow," Isobel says. She watches Heather walk away, unable to shake the dread accumulating in her chest.

Chapter Eleven

Jade climbed the stairs with Cliché at her heels. He continued on into her bedroom while she stopped in the bathroom to brush her teeth. She owed Delany a return phone call and had put it off long enough. Today would be the perfect day—Delany's birthday.

She paced across her bedroom as she waited for Delany to answer. Excitement mixed with dread coursed through her. Dread? Not exactly dread. It was more like…she didn't know exactly.

"Hello," Delany answered on the fourth ring.

"Happy birthday."

"Thanks. It's good to hear from you."

Jade mentally kicked herself for not calling sooner.

"What are you up to? Did you do something fun for your birthday?" She put the phone on speaker and laid it on the dresser so she could change into her pajamas. The ball in the pit of her stomach dissolved with the sound of Delany's voice.

"Abby took me out for dinner and then to my sister's for cake. And at the moment, I'm up to my armpits in soap."

"That sounds like quite the bath. I hope you're getting good and clean." She slipped out of her clothes, then tugged her pajama bottoms on, followed by her nightshirt.

Delany laughed. Jade truly did like the sound of it. "No. I'm making soap."

"What do you mean, you're making soap? Like from scratch? I don't even know how one goes about doing that. How do you make soap?" She sat on the bed and absentmindedly stroked Cliché until he got tired of it and jumped down.

"Yeah, from scratch. It's made from lye and fat, like olive oil, coconut oil, or beef tallow. Sort of like the suet you might put out for the birds in the winter."

Jade was impressed but confused. "Wait a minute. You make soap from lye, like the stuff you put down a clogged drain, and oil? No way. I can't believe that's what makes soap." Delany must be messing with her.

"It is. I add essential or fragrance oils. This batch is lavender mint. I even put some bits of real lavender in it. I'll give you some next time I see you."

Next time I see you, Jade repeated in her head. Would she be seeing Delany again? More than likely, yes. She went to Rochester every few months, at least, and if they were going to be friends, wouldn't it make sense to see her? Against her will, she found herself looking forward to it.

"Great. I would love some of your soap. Am I keeping you from it? Do you need to get back to it?"

"No, I can talk while I work. I'm about done for the night anyway. So what were you up to today?"

"Nothing as interesting as making soap. I played tennis at the club and mostly hung out with Cliché today."

"Huh? Cliché?"

"Oh, that's my cat." As if on cue he jumped back onto her lap.

"Interesting name."

"You know it's so cliché for lesbians to have cats. I thought it fit."

Delany laughed again. "I love it. Hey, I was thinking of taking a ride your way next Saturday. There's a store in Buffalo that sells soap supplies. If I do, what would you think about getting together? As friends," she quickly added.

"Sure," Jade said, without even thinking. She smiled at the thought. "As friends."

❖

"Friends," Isobel says to Tomas. "We are friends. I like her." She has trouble reading the expression on his face. Isobel continues to pluck the green beans from the vines and add them to her basket. She wipes the sweat from her forehead with her wrist. The sun is high in the sky, and the kerchief tied on her head offers little protection.

"I worry, Bellie," he says. "Her brother does not like her spending time with you, and he could cause you trouble."

"No need to worry. She is careful when she comes to visit. He need not know."

"You must not let Uncle know of your friendship, either," Tomas adds. "He would not take kindly to it. He tries to present himself at a higher position in society than he is. Your mixing with the likes of that wealthy girl would bring attention to our lack."

"Only you know, Tomas." And Heather's friend Maura, Isobel thinks. She wishes Heather had never told Maura about them. She wishes Heather was her secret, and her secret alone.

She looks at the rows of beans yet to pick for the day. She must hurry along if she wants to get to the stream to meet Heather at the hour of which they spoke. She can wash in the stream before Heather arrives.

"Go on," Tomas says to her. "I will finish up here. Go see your friend. I know you've a mind to."

She smiles at her big brother. "Thank you," she says, and lifts the basket of beans to put on the wagon.

"Leave it," he says. "I shall take care of it. Off with you."

CHAPTER TWELVE

The anticipation of seeing Jade again filled Delany's heart and head, making her feel somehow lighter as she drove to Buffalo. This was how Isobel felt about seeing Heather again, she thought. Delany knew there would be no kissing or touching between her and Jade, but knowing it and fully accepting it were two different things. She had hopes, but no expectations that Jade would change her mind.

Delany was still getting glimpses of what she was sure was a past life with Jade. Some came in through her dreams and some played out in her mind like a movie when she was fully awake. She was learning to experience them while still being fully present with whatever she was doing. Abby's words came back to her often. *Even if you did have a past life with her, that doesn't mean you should be having this life with her.*

She tried to sort out her current feelings for Jade versus the feelings she had as Isobel for Heather. When she did have bits of memories, they came with the intense feelings Isobel must have experienced. But she was sure her feelings for Jade were real and not imagined or left over from that life. Well, almost sure. She really hadn't spent that much time with her, so it was hard to tell.

But it didn't matter if her feelings were real or not if Jade didn't return them. She wished Jade would give them a chance. To date each other, simple as that.

Maybe she should broach the subject. Feel Jade out and see if she would agree. No. Jade had made it perfectly clear that if they were to be anything, it would be *friends*. Nothing more. If Delany pushed it, Jade would back away entirely. Delany knew it.

"Turn slight right at exit fifty-one in one mile," Delany's GPS told her.

Butterflies took flight in her stomach. "Stop," she said, looking down at the offending body part. "This is ridiculous. Friends. We are just friends. Put your thoughts and feelings on the shelf, and have a nice time. Period."

The butterflies made another brief appearance as she pulled into Jade's driveway. She willed herself to relax and knocked on the door.

Jade answered, dressed in a T-shirt and form-fitting jeans. Casual but sexy. "Wow, it's colder outside than I thought," she said, after letting Delany in and giving her a brief hug.

"Did you forget you live in western New York, where spring doesn't actually arrive until late May at best, and anything up to that point is iffy?"

Jade chuckled. "Apparently I did. I'm going to run upstairs and change. Make yourself comfortable."

Delany looked around the living room. The lack of pictures on the wall or personal knickknacks was obvious. A few magazines lay neatly across a glass coffee table directly in front of the plain brown couch, which matched the plain brown chair by the wall. A flat-screen TV sat in the corner on top of a small bookshelf. Delany meandered over and read the titles of the few books there. Most were books on business or tennis. A few were self-help and relationship books...*How to Love Yourself, Why Do I Do That, I'm Okay, You're Okay.*

Geez, I hope she's okay, Delany thought.

She heard a low rumble and realized it was purring. She looked down at the cat rubbing against her leg. "Hey there," she said. "You must be Cliché."

"Holy cow," Jade said, coming back into the room. "You must be special. He doesn't have much use for anyone unless he thinks he can get something. You don't have catnip in your pocket, do you?"

"That's not catnip in my pocket," Delany said. "I'm just happy to see you."

"Ha ha. You're very funny."

"Funny is my middle name. Okay, that's a lie. It's actually Mildred. But I'm thinking of changing it to Funny. What do you think? Delany Funny Payton."

"I like it." Jade had changed into a snug sweatshirt. "Mildred? Your middle name is really Mildred?" She laughed.

Delany found herself smiling. "Hey, don't laugh. It's a perfectly good name. There are a lot of wonderful women named Mildred."

"Oh yeah? Name one."

"Mildred Pierce."

"She was a fictional character."

"I might be a fictional character myself. You never know." The light banter was just the thing to send any remaining butterflies on their way.

"Oh, I know you're real all right. I've experienced you myself. You felt very real to me when I kissed you."

A jolt of electricity shot through Delany at Jade's words and the memory of Jade's kisses.

A blush crept up Jade's face. "Um, maybe we should get going, Delany Mildred."

"Hey, that's Delany Funny to you." She willed her body to release the sexual feelings that had wrapped themselves around her.

"Sorry. Maybe we should get going, Delany Funny."

"Much better. I thought we could get some breakfast before we go to the soap shop. What do you think?"

Jade grabbed a jacket from the hall closet. Delany reached for it to help her slip it on but then thought better of it.

"I know just the place, unless you have somewhere in mind." She locked the door behind them. "Okay if I drive?"

"This is your town, so lead the way, m'lady." Delany shook off a feeling of déjà vu and followed Jade out to her car.

The diner was only a few blocks away. "Don't you love the smell of this place?" Jade said.

"Mmm," Delany agreed, taking in the mingled scents of fresh coffee, baked goods, and bacon.

A waitress in a pink uniform waltzed by with a coffeepot. *Who dresses like that anymore?* The whole place had that 50s vibe to it. "Go ahead and sit anywhere you want, Jade," she said.

"Jade? Eat here often?" Delany asked, following her past rows of tables to a booth by the window.

"I do." She slid onto the green vinyl seat.

Delany sat on the opposite side and picked up the menu.

Jade didn't touch hers.

"Coffee, hon?" the waitress asked Delany, already pouring Jade's.

"Sure," Delany answered.

"Know what you want yet?"

Delany looked at the waitress, then at Jade. "Um, no. Do you?" she asked Jade.

"Yes. I get the eight greats special. Two eggs, two sausages, two pieces of bacon, and two pancakes. Oh, and toast."

"That makes ten things, not eight."

"We don't count the toast," the waitress said, with a smile.

"All right. I'll have the same. Eggs scrambled, please."

"Sure thing, honey," she said, and was gone.

"How's your job going?" Delany asked Jade, trying to make small talk.

"Great. On Friday an irate customer demanded to talk to a supervisor and then proceeded to called me a fucking retard when I got on the phone."

"Oh my God. What did you say?"

"I said, in my nicest voice—'cause that's the one we're

supposed to use, no matter what. I said, 'That isn't politically correct, sir. The R-word is offensive.'" She paused for dramatic effect. "So he says, 'Lady, you're so right. Forgive me. You're fucking mentally challenged. Or if that isn't politically correct enough for you, how about you're fucking intellectually disabled? Now fix my goddamn bill.'"

"Crap. Is that the kind of people you have to deal with? That must be tough."

"It is tough. But what doesn't kill us makes us stronger—or psychotic. I'm leaning toward the latter."

Delany chuckled. She loved Jade's sense of humor. "What did you end up doing?"

"He had jacked his heat way up and forgot to lower it. There wasn't anything I could do."

"I think I'll stick to teaching. That's not to say that I haven't had to deal with an angry student or ten over their grades." Delany opened and poured three small containers of half-and-half into her coffee and stirred it. "Why don't you want a relationship?" Delany surprised even herself when the question slipped out of her mouth. She'd had no intention of asking it. "Never mind. You don't have to answer that."

"When we're free of the desire for another person, they can never deceive or hurt us," Jade said matter-of-factly. "I guess I choose to be free of the desire."

What? "How can you choose to not desire someone? The desire's either there or it's not," Delany said, a little louder than she had intended.

Jade shrugged, leaving Delany more confused than ever. She didn't know whether to push the issue or let it go. Part of her wanted to push it, to show Jade how making a decision like that could impact her life, what she'd be missing. But letting it go would probably lead to a more pleasant day. And Delany was determined for it to be a pleasant day—for both of them.

Chapter Thirteen

"Smell this." Delany held a small bottle near Jade's nose and waved her hand, sending the fragrance in Jade's direction. "Do you like it?"

She did. "Wow. Yes. What's is it?"

"It's a mixture of…Geez, there's a lot of stuff in here, hazelnuts, chocolate, caramel, vanilla, patchouli, and green chypre. Let's see…" Delany held the bottle up. "The name of it is Angel Sent. This would work great in soap."

"What's green chypre?"

"It's made from the milk of a yak."

"Really?"

Delany laughed. "No, not really. I made that up. I have no idea."

"Jerk." Jade couldn't help but laugh along. She was really enjoying the day—well, aside from that question about not wanting a relationship. Wasting nine years on the last one had taught her a lot. And it certainly *was* possible to choose to be free of desire. Or at least bury it so deep that even the worms couldn't get to it. She shook the thoughts from her mind and picked up another sampler bottle. "Lucky Jade," she read on the label. She unscrewed the top and took a whiff. The pungent order wafted to her nose and hung there like a rotting piece of fruit. The smell remained in her nostrils even after she closed the bottle. "Yuck."

"Guess Lucky Jade isn't so lucky after all, huh?" Delany said, with a grin.

"Not funny. We may have to change your middle name again." She grinned back. "Maybe back to Mildred." Delany reached out and tickled Jade's ribs.

Jade pulled back from Delany as a sense of fear enveloped her. It felt familiar. Too familiar. Why? It felt familiar in the same way kissing Delany had. She hadn't realized at the time, too caught up in the physical passion that she had been craving. But it came back to her now.

"Sorry," Delany said.

"No. No problem. I wasn't expecting that, and it startled me. That's all." She turned her back to Delany and pretended to look at the bottles on the shelf, silently reprimanding herself for acting like an idiot.

Delany touched her shoulder, her fingers warm and comforting. "Really. I didn't mean anything by that. I was goofing around, being a jerk."

She turned around and mustered up a smile. "You're not a jerk. I overreacted." And she had no idea why. There seemed to be a lot of things she was having trouble figuring out lately. One thing she knew for sure. She had to keep this woman at arm's length. She couldn't quite put her finger on it, but it could somehow mean heartbreak for her.

"I'm going to pay for these. I'm getting the Angel Sent and this stuff." She lifted the hand-held shopping basket. "Anything special you want me to make you?"

Jade shook her head. "You don't have to make me anything."

"I know I don't *have* to. It wouldn't be any fun if I *had* to. I want to. Maybe next time you're in town we can make soap together. If you want," she quickly added.

Jade still felt bad about overreacting to Delany's good-natured tickling. "Um, sure. I would like that." She couldn't help but notice Delany's face light up.

"Great." Delany started toward the register, stopped, and

turned back. "Sure there isn't anything else you wanted me to get?"

"I'm sure. And thanks." Now it was Jade who was smiling. Delany certainly was thoughtful. She would make a great partner one day—for someone else.

Jade shut the trunk of the car once Delany's purchases were safely inside. "Where to now?"

"That was all I had on my list for today." Delany buckled her seat belt.

"What would you think about stopping at the nursing home and visiting with my uncle for a bit? I haven't been there for several days." There weren't too many people she would have asked to accompany her to the nursing home. Her uncle could be confusing and even a little disturbing. She was confident Delany would have no problem with it.

"Sure. I would love to meet him."

"Then maybe we could go back to my place and watch a movie or something? I'm sure Cliché would love to see you again."

Delany tapped a finger on her chin. "Hmm. Well, okay. But only for the sake of your cat. I would hate to disappoint the little guy. Nothing worse than a disappointed puss..." She stopped. "Sorry."

Jade glanced at Delany and laughed.

"Are you laughing at me?"

"I'm laughing at how red your face is. You don't have to walk on eggshells around me. You can say the word 'pussy'—at least when referring to my cat. Although I know you weren't, with your little joke." Far more amused than offended, she added, "But it's okay."

"Well, there is nothing worse than a disappointed pussy—cat."

Jade shook her head. "What am I going to do with you?" She pointed a finger at Delany. "Do not answer that."

Delany hooked her own finger around Jade's and gave it a

little tug. "I won't answer it, but I can think of lots of stuff you can do with me."

Jade pulled her hand back and turned her head away from Delany to hide her smile. She looked over her shoulder to check for traffic and pulled out.

"What? You said not to answer, and I didn't answer."

"I know." But she had some answers of her own.

❖

"Jade. My favorite niece." Uncle Willy gave her a tight hug.

"I'm your only niece, Uncle." She kissed him on the cheek.

"Oh. I thought you had a sister. What was her name? Oh yeah. Millie, isn't it?" He turned to Delany and took her hand. "Is that you, Millie?"

Delany looked helplessly at Jade. She didn't have any experience with this sort of thing.

"No, Uncle. This is my friend, Delany."

"Well, where's Millie, then?" he asked, obviously fixating on it.

"Mom's at home. She'll be visiting you soon. Can you say hello to Delany?"

He still held Delany's hand and shook it gently before giving it a squeeze. "Of course. Where are my manners? Hello."

"It's so nice to meet you," Delany said. What an honor to spend time with Jade's uncle. She knew how important he was to her.

"Likewise."

"Uncle Willy, let's go sit outside in the sunshine."

"Fine idea," Uncle Willy said, and followed her out, Delany close behind.

Jade led the way to an enclosed garden set up in the center of the facility. It probably allowed the residents the opportunity to spend time outside without the risk of them wandering away, Delany reasoned.

"Jade," he said, once they were all comfortably seated on the cushioned chairs arranged in a semicircle in the shade of a small ash tree, "I've been thinking that you need to get glasses."

Jade looked momentarily baffled. "You mean eyeglasses?"

"Yeah, yeah. Those."

Jade turned her head and winked at Delany. "I don't think I need them. There's nothing wrong with my eyes."

Uncle Willy continued. "My friend Dave has glasses. Remember my friend Dave?"

"Um...he worked with you at the bank, didn't he?"

"Yeah. He had glasses." A pause ensued. "I wonder if I have his address."

"Do you want to get in touch with him?"

"No. He died, and he didn't leave a forwarding address." Uncle Willy chuckled at his own joke, which Delany appreciated. "But I used to talk to his son all the time."

"I can try to get in touch with his son, if you like."

"No, it's okay." Uncle Willy tapped his chin. "I'm just thinking you need glasses."

"Okay. I'll schedule an exam." She patted her uncle's knee and shared a conspiratorial eyebrow waggle with Delany.

Watching how patient Jade was with her uncle moved her up another notch in Delany's mind.

"So, I was thinking," Uncle Willy continued. "I might get in touch with Dave's son."

"How come, Uncle?"

"I want to ask him if you need glasses."

Delany suppressed her urge to laugh. But Jade didn't. Her laugh was soft and tender.

"I love you," she said, leaning in to give him a squeeze. "And when I go to the eye doctor, I'll be sure to ask him if I need glasses."

"The eye doctor," Uncle Willy said, as though the conversation wasn't one he himself had started. "Good idea. I wish I'd thought of that."

❖

"You're so good with your uncle," Delany said, following Jade into her house. She was having a very good day.

"Thanks." Jade took Delany's jacket and hung it up in the hall closet, doing the same with her own.

"It must be hard for you seeing him like that."

"It's strange. Dementia robs a person of who they are. He had this whole life but can only remember bits and pieces. Yet things that happened in the life he can't remember affect aspects of his life now." Jade shook her head. "That life was important. Even if he can't remember it. Know what I mean?" She led the way to the living room and motioned for Delany to sit down on the couch.

"I do." She was feeling much the same way about the past life they had shared. It was important, even if she only remembered bits and pieces and Jade didn't remember it at all. She was tempted to say something, to tell Jade everything she had remembered and learned. She opened her mouth, but nothing came out. No. She couldn't tell her. Not now. It would send her running, and Delany felt like they were just starting to really get to know each other.

"Ready to watch a movie?" Jade asked.

Delany nodded. She found herself staring at Jade's delightful rear end as Jade walked across the room to the TV. Delany looked up quickly when Jade turned around, remote in hand. "Um, what did you say?" she asked her.

"I didn't say anything," Jade answered.

"Oh. I thought you said something."

"Nope. But nice try."

Obviously, she hadn't gotten away with her ogling. She smiled.

Jade smiled back and sat down on the opposite side of the couch. It didn't escape Delany's notice. She wondered if she could get away with moving closer and decided to stay where she was. Besides, Cliché was curled up on her lap. The best way to win Jade's heart might be through her cat. He looked up at her as if he could read her mind, yawned, and jumped down. "See ya, buddy," Delany called after him. *And thanks.*

"What would you like to watch?" Jade asked. "I've got Netflix or we could order something off Amazon."

"How about *Braveheart*?" She'd been meaning to watch it for, um…research?

"Mel Gibson fan?"

"No. Scottish fan."

"Are you Scottish?"

"Not now I'm not."

Jade turned toward her. "What does that mean?"

Delany realized what she said and smiled. "Nothing. I've been there lately." *Damn. Can't keep slipping like this.*

"You have? When?"

"Actually, I've never been there—actually." She rummaged through her brain for words, knowing she probably sounded stupid. "I mean I've had an interest in it lately. I didn't mean I've actually been there. Actually." She covered with a smile. She hoped it worked.

Jade rolled her eyes. She did a quick search on Netflix and found what they were looking for.

Delany watched the movie with great interest, looking more at the landscapes and scenery than the actors for the most part, although she did notice their clothes. She wanted to know if anything would seem familiar to her. Some of it did. There were little bits and pieces, especially the cliffs and rolling hills and how green the grass was. The houses didn't seem to be quite right, though. She thought there should have been more wood and less stone. She found herself getting emotional at times and even had a few tears escape. She did her best to brush them away without Jade noticing.

"I don't remember any men actually wearing kilts like that."

Delany didn't realize she'd spoken aloud until Jade said, "What?"

"I was just mumbling to myself. Nothing important." *Oh boy, shouldn't have said anything.*

"What did you say, though?" Jade asked again.

"I said"—Delany cleared her throat—"I don't remember kilts…" Again she considered telling Jade about her visions and the past-life regression. But only for a moment. She felt like she was lying by omission, but she was afraid Jade would think she was nuts. She didn't want that. "In my, um, research about Scotland. They seem out of place." It was close enough to the truth. She had done some research since this whole thing started.

"It's Scotland. I thought the men wore kilts," Jade said.

"Yeah. I guess so. It doesn't seem right. Did you notice what year this takes place? Not the year the movie was made, but the year the story takes place?"

"I didn't. I think they showed it at the beginning but I don't remember what it said. Do you want me to go back to the beginning?"

"No. It would be a pain to try to find our place again."

"Want me to look it up on my laptop?"

Delany felt foolish for asking, but curiosity was starting to get the better of her. "Would you mind?"

Jade paused the movie and ran upstairs. She came down a few minutes later with her computer and sat down. This time next to Delany.

"Okay, let's see…" Jade typed: *braveheart year story takes place* in the Google search box and clicked on the first link that came up. "According to Wikipedia—1995 historical drama—starring Mel Gibson—portrays William Wallace, a thirteenth-century Scottish warrior…"

"So, it was the 1200s. A couple hundred years earlier."

"Earlier than what?"

"Nothing. I was wondering when men actually started wearing kilts." *I must sound like a lunatic.*

Jade gave her a sideways glance before clicking on another link. "According to this site, the movie is not historically accurate. Interesting."

"Does it talk about the kilts?"

"My God, woman," Jade said, with a smirk. "You seem to be obsessed with kilts."

Jade read the article aloud. Most of the inaccuracies had to do with the main character himself or the battle scenes, but Jade did find something on the clothing. "Hey, you were right. Kilts didn't become popular for men to wear until well into the seventeenth century." She bumped Delany's shoulder with her own. "I'm impressed. How did you know that?"

Delany had no way of explaining without sounding crazy. The only thing she knew for sure was that there were no kilts on any of the men in any of the glimpses she'd had of their past life. She simply shrugged.

Jade seemed appeased enough that she put her computer down and used the remote to continue the movie. She never moved back to her spot on the other end of the couch, and Delany was glad to have her close by.

It was dark by the time Delany was ready to leave. Actually, she didn't want to leave at all. The day with Jade was wonderful. She knew it would be a while before she would see her again, so she took her time putting her shoes and jacket on. "Let's keep in touch," she said.

"Absolutely. I had a nice time. Thanks for inviting me along on your soap-buying adventure."

"Anytime." *How about next weekend?* Delany thought, but didn't say out loud. She pulled Jade in for a hug, half expecting her to resist, but she didn't. Delany held her a beat longer than she thought she should have. She just didn't want to let go.

"Thanks," Jade said.

Her warm breath on Delany's neck sent shivers down her spine. She let go and took a step back. "For what?"

"For everything."

Delany wanted to hug her again but opened the door instead. A blast of cold air rushed in, cooling off the heat burning inside her. She pulled the collar of her coat up higher, nodded to Jade, and forced herself out into the chilly night.

❖

Jade stood in the doorway despite the cold and watched her drive away, giving a small wave as Delany pulled out of the driveway. She closed the door and leaned against it. Cliché rubbed against her legs. "Oh, sure. Your friend leaves and suddenly you like me again? If there's one thing I don't need, it's a fair-weather friend."

Friend. She hoped she and Delany could really be friends. She knew Delany wanted more, even though she didn't come right out and say it. Maybe she was being foolish. Maybe it wasn't possible to be friends after the way they started. She didn't know, but she wanted to try.

She truly did enjoy Delany's company and the way she made her laugh. They had laughed a lot today. Maybe she would take a trip to Rochester sooner rather than later and spend the day making soap, of all things, with her.

❖

"Irving made arrangements for me to marry." Heather sobs as she sits with Isobel at the edge of the stream. The overcast sky seems as dark as Isobel feels.

"No. No. No," Isobel screams. "It cannot be true. Please." Unbearable pressure squeezes her heart. She has great difficulty catching her breath.

"I told him I would not, and he said I had no choice. I cannot possibly marry and be moved so far away from here." She takes Isobel's hand. "So far away from you."

"What did he say?" The panic swallowing her breath makes it hard to speak the words. She doesn't fight the tears that spring to her eyes.

"He said that he is the man of the family, and I must do what he says. Oh, Isobel, I just cannot!"

Isobel pulls Heather into her arms and sobs into Heather's shoulder. She can't tell her it will be all right, for surely it will not. Her mind races. How can they stop this? Can she hide Heather? Can they run away together? Surely she can't leave Tomas. How would they live? What would they do? Too many questions without answers.

Isobel rocks side to side holding tight to Heather, afraid to let her go. After a long while, their tears subside.

"We must think of a plan," Heather says. "Please, we must think."

"When is this set to happen?" Isobel asks.

"Irving says soon. I know not the day."

Isobel fears their carefree days of love are soon to be over forever. Her heart can't bear the weight of it. She wipes a tear that drips from Heather's eye. She kisses her forehead, her nose, her lips. She is swept away with urgency, for she may never kiss these lips again.

Heather responds to her with equal ferocity. They are so intertwined, lips, tongues, hearts, that Isobel feels in this moment they can never be torn apart.

But the thought is in vain. Heather is suddenly ripped from her arms. Irving's meaty hand is wrapped around Heather's arm, and she stands almost limp beside him.

"You little wench," he bellows at Isobel. "You shall not steal the innocence from my sister. I tell you now that I will see you die before that happens."

"No!" Heather screams at him. She struggles to free herself from his grip. He slaps her across the face with much force. An angry red welt raises up on her cheek.

Isobel leaps up and lunges at him. She's no match, and with one thrust of his arm, she is sent flailing backward and her head hits the ground. Hard.

She hears Heather scream but can't gather herself together enough to get back onto her feet. The taste of blood makes her gag. Against her will, her eyes close. When she is able to open them again, Irving is dragging Heather away by the arm. He appears unfazed as she beats her fists against his arm and chest. He's practically lifting her feet off the ground as he makes away with her. Darkness closes in around Isobel's senses, and she fades out of consciousness.

"Isobel." Tomas runs to her and helps her in. He guides her to a chair and eases her down. "What has happened?"

"I fell off a rock," she lies. She knows if she tells him the truth he'll go after Irving. She also knows that if he does, he might well end up dead. Lying is the only way to protect him.

"What were you doing?" He pours water on a clean rag.

Isobel winces as he dabs at her face, gently wiping away the dirt and blood.

"Climbing."

"You are lucky you were not killed. Where was Heather? I thought you were meeting her." He pulls some muddied straw from her hair and holds it in front of her face. "You must have hit the ground very hard."

"I did."

"Heather? Where was she when all this was taking place?" he repeated.

"She had gone home already."

"Bellie, you must stop doing this sort of thing. I don't want to lose you."

Isobel begins to cry.

"Oh, come now. I do not mean anything by that. I want you to be safe is all."

"I do not know what to do. Irving is marrying Heather off to a nobleman. I cannot bear the thought of her marrying and going away." She covers her face with her hands. Her heart is breaking, and nothing in this world will ever make it right.

Tomas squats down in front of her and pulls her hands down. He holds them in his and looks up into her eyes. "I know she is your friend and you care about her. She's late getting married, as are you, I might add. It is natural for her brother to look after her that way and arrange a husband."

"I am never getting married," she says through gritted teeth. "And you cannot make me. And Irving cannot make Heather." Her words are hollow in her ears, for she knows Irving can and will make her get married.

"I would never do that if it was not your wish. You know that. But I am afraid Heather may have no say in who or when she marries. Her brother will see to that. He has her best interest at heart, I am sure."

The words stab at her already shredded heart. Surely Tomas cannot believe it's all right for Heather to be forced into marriage? Can he not see how much she loves Heather? Can he not see how much they love each other? No, he does not see, because Isobel has never let him see. She dare not tell him now. She fears it would be looked upon as wrong. None of that matters now. Irving has taken Heather away and Isobel will never see her again. Fresh tears pour from her eyes and crushing pain squeezes her chest as her heart shatters into pieces. How will she ever survive?

Chapter Fourteen

Delany woke with a start. She wiped drips of sweat from her forehead, expecting to find blood. The memory of the dream stayed strong in her mind, not like normal dreams that break into pieces and float away when you turn on the light.

Oh my God, I'm losing Heather. Delany shook her head. She never had Heather. Isobel had Heather. Delany had Jade. No, she didn't have Jade, not really. She never had.

She sat upright in bed and tried to clear her head and sort out the dream from reality. The dream seemed so real. Felt so real. Her pillow was wet from tears.

She looked at the clock. One in the morning. Too late to call Abby and talk to her about this. She couldn't call Jade and tell her, that was for sure. Did Jade feel any of this? Feel any of the same connection Delany felt? She doubted it. If Jade did, she was doing a great job hiding it.

Delany had no one she could turn to or call at this hour. She was alone in this. There was no one in the bed to hold her and tell her it was just a dream. She knew it wasn't.

She pulled her journal and a pen from her nightstand drawer.

Dear Jade,
    I know you aren't going to believe this, but I had you once—in another life. I know. Unbelievable, right?

You were taken from me, snatched from my arms. They felt empty without you. They feel empty without you now. What are these feelings that I have for you? Are they even real? Do I want you now because I had you before? Did I lose you in that lifetime? Can I ever truly have you in this one? I wanted to let you know the truth. And I do believe that is the truth. I hope you believe it.
Delany

Delany closed the journal and replaced it in the drawer, knowing she would never send it. Writing it down was the only way to try to get it out and stop it from bouncing around in her head for the rest of the night.

❖

Jade turned over in bed and looked at the clock on her nightstand. It was a little after one. What the heck? Waking up in the middle of the night and finding it impossible to fall back asleep wasn't something she usually did.

She rolled out of bed, slipped on her robe, and headed downstairs. Cliché was sleeping on the bottom step and she held the railing so she could step over him without tripping.

She passed by the television on her way to the kitchen and recalled her evening with Delany. For some reason, that movie, *Braveheart*, had gotten to Delany. More than once Jade saw her wiping tears from her cheeks. Jade pretended not to notice. Not that there weren't some sad parts in the movie—there definitely were—but Delany didn't seem to be crying during those times.

Jade peered into the refrigerator, closed the door without taking anything out, and headed back to the living room. She plopped down on the sofa. She couldn't lose the restless feeling she had woken up with. Maybe restless wasn't the right word. It bordered on anxiety, a problem Jade had never really had before.

Sure, she had her moments here and there. Who didn't? But this feeling was unusual for her, and she couldn't quite figure it out.

❖

Delany turned off the light and lay in the dark for quite a while before sleep finally overtook her.

"I got word from the men in town," Tomas says.

"Tell me," Isobel pleads, afraid to hear his answer. She shivers despite the warm summer air.

"Irving is sending Heather to Banchory to be married in two weeks' time."

Isobel sinks to the ground. "No," she cries out. "No." This can't be true. It can't. Her heart can't take any more pain. She wishes for it to stop beating, for without Heather there is no reason for it to pump.

"Isobel, there is nothing to be done." He tries to help her to her feet but her body won't cooperate. Surely her bones have dissolved and there is nothing left to hold her up.

"Leave me be," she pleads.

"I cannot leave you like this. At least come inside." He paces to the cabin and back to Isobel. "Please, Isobel."

She pulls herself up into a sitting position and looks up at him, her face wet from tears. She knows this is just the beginning of them, and they may never stop for all her life. For what is her life without Heather? Nothing.

"Come inside, Isobel," Tomas says again.

She rises slowly to her feet and enters her childhood home. The home where her parents lived and where she learned of their deaths. The home she and Heather came to often, to talk and laugh and be alone. Alone. That was what her life would be about now—being alone. And Heather—her life would be different, too. She wouldn't be alone. She would be married, taken at the pleasure of her husband whenever he pleased. Forced to bear his children.

The thought of it all is too much to take and Isobel collapses. Tomas catches her and helps her to the bed. "Rest," he tells her.

He must think she is making a fuss over nothing—over losing a friend. But Heather is more than a friend. She is Isobel's life. Isobel's life is leaving in two weeks. She is too tired to think about it. Too tired to exist.

She closes her eyes, but they still leak pain that drips down her cheeks.

Chapter Fifteen

A bby wrapped her arms around Delany and gave her a tight squeeze. "I'm so glad to see you. Come on into my office." She led the way with Delany close behind.

The smell of jasmine and vanilla filled the air. A massage table covered by a clean white sheet sat in the center of the room. Two folding chairs and a small table holding various rocks, gems, and candles lined one wall. A colorful banner with the seven chakras represented on it hung above the table, a dream catcher next to that. "I was surprised when I looked at my schedule and saw you'd called to make an appointment." Abby leaned against the edge of the massage table and motioned for Delany to sit in the plush office chair facing her. "What's going on?"

"I'm thinking it's time for some Reiki. I'm feeling ungrounded. This Isobel and Heather stuff is getting to me, and it hurts my heart to feel Isobel's pain."

Abby rubbed her shoulder. "I know, honey. It's like you have to go through the pain of losing her all over again. I hope it worked out for them...for your sake."

"Me too. Speaking of pain—I've got pain in the back of my calf." Delany rubbed the area. "It's not like a charley horse. It's hard to describe."

"Did you bruise it or hit it on something?"

"Not as far as I can remember. My doctor couldn't find any reason for it."

"Okay, lie down. Let's see what we can do." She patted the table.

Delany stretched out on her back and Abby adjusted a pillow under her head.

"What's going on with Jade? Anything?" Abby asked.

"We had a great time when I was there on Saturday, and that's about it. I haven't called her since I got back and she hasn't called me." Delany decided to leave it in Jade's hands, but that didn't stop her from being disappointed by the lack of contact. "Have you heard from her?"

"We exchanged a few texts. Nothing really." Abby rolled up her sleeves.

Delany wasn't surprised. She closed her eyes, used to this routine and everything Abby was going to do.

Abby placed her hand above Delany's head without making contact. Her hands "scanned" Delany from head to toe, going down each leg separately, "feeling" for any areas that might need attention. Fully committed to the principles of Reiki, she used the transfer of energy from herself to Delany for physical, mental, emotional, and spiritual healing.

Abby sat in the office chair and placed her hands on the top of Delany's head, the crown chakra—Abby had explained the seven chakras the first time she'd worked on Delany.

Heat radiated from Abby's hands, and a feeling of peace enveloped Delany. She sank into the feeling and was close to drifting off when Abby finished. Even her calf pain had lessened considerably.

"How do you feel now?" Abby asked once Delany was back in an upright position.

"Much better. Thanks."

"Tell me what's going on with you?"

Over the past several weeks, Delany had felt like her life had been split in two. There was the life she was really living and the life story that was being lived her head—the story of Isobel and Heather. That story seemed as real as this one. "I'm having more flashbacks. Waking up at night with dreams, having flashes of them during the day, living them in my mind." It was tiring.

"Are you having trouble telling the difference between what's real and what's not?"

"It's all real. But if you mean can I sort it out, yes. I know which life is which. The past life is sort of like watching a movie, except I can feel it."

"What do you want to do about it?"

"I'm not sure there is anything I can do. An exorcism maybe." Delany hopped off the table. "I'm kidding."

Abby didn't respond.

"You're supposed to laugh."

"Ha ha," Abby said. "I'm worried about you."

"I'm okay. This is just different from anything I've been through before. I actually don't want it to stop. At least not until I know how it turned out. I want to know that Isobel and Heather got their happily ever after."

"And what now? What about Jade? Are you still chasing after her?"

Delany frowned. "I'm not chasing after her." She was taking great pains to make sure of that. Why didn't Abby get that?

"You know what I mean."

Delany wasn't pursuing her. Period. She hadn't even called her since she got home from Buffalo. Not that she hadn't thought about it several times. Okay, more than several. She had even clicked Jade's name in her contact list a few times and then hit cancel before the call had a chance to connect. She did her best to put Jade out of her mind every time she crept in—which was a lot. Yeah, she was still hung up on Jade, but she definitely wasn't chasing her.

"Well?" Abby asked again.

Apparently, she wasn't going to drop this. "I'm not. There's no point in that. She made it clear where she stands, and I have to respect her wishes." It didn't mean she had to like them, though. "I am perfectly happy being her friend." Was that an out-and-out lie or just a partial truth?

"Good. I don't want to see you get hurt, Delany."

Delany shook her head. "Me neither." She really hoped she wasn't heading in that direction.

Isobel can't keep her mind on her work. All she can think about is Heather. She scans the crowd of people at the marketplace for the hundredth time trying to find sight of her or Irving. She sees neither.

An elderly woman dressed in rags thumps her on the arm. "I said, I would like six of these," she says, pushing a handful of carrots toward her.

"So sorry. Yes, of course." Isobel takes the woman's coin.

She has neither seen nor heard from Heather since that awful day when Irving dragged her away. Heather is to be married. She doesn't want to believe it to be true. She has stayed up at night thinking of a plan. Running away together might be their only hope. She must talk to Heather. But how? Even if she does show up at the marketplace today, surely she will be with Irving, and he will keep strict control of her. She knows where Heather lives but does not dare go for fear of losing her life.

A proper young woman waltzes up to the selling cart. She hands Isobel a piece of paper and then waltzes away. Isobel looks at the fine linen paper and flawless black ink. She can't read and has no idea of what is written there. Tomas would be no help, for he can't read either. Only nobility, and sometimes the wealthy, are taught to read. She knows of no one that is such a person—except Heather. Surely this must be from Heather. She flushes with heat. The girl who delivered it was probably her friend, Maura.

She must find someone to read the letter to her. But who? Who could she find to read it as well as be able to trust with what might be written there?

That was the last vision Delany had of Isobel in the past two weeks. She should have felt relief, but she was starting to feel panicked. It couldn't end where it was. She had to know what happened. There was no way to research it. It had to come from somewhere inside her, or maybe beyond her. She wasn't sure.

Abby had suggested that maybe Delany should go back and talk to Valerie. Not for another past-life regression, but this time as a psychic to see if she might have any insight.

Delany sat at her desk at school, staring at the phone in her hand, working up the nerve to call to make the appointment. It rang, startling her, and causing her to nearly dropped it on the floor. A quick look at the caller ID told her it was Jade. For a moment she thought she should let it go to voicemail—make Jade wait for a call back from her for a change. She hadn't heard from her since the day they spent together in Buffalo. Of course, Delany hadn't called her either. She was hoping Jade would make the first move. It had taken longer than Delany had hoped, but Jade was calling now, and that counted for something.

"Hello," Delany answered, just before it went to voicemail.

"Hi." Jade sounded cheerful. "How ya doing?"

"Good. You?"

"I was wondering when you might be making soap again. Maybe I could spend the day with you. I think it would be fun watching you."

Delany was caught off guard. She had no immediate plans to make soap but would certainly change that if it meant spending the day with Jade. She leaned back in her chair. "Oh no. That's not the way it works."

"What do you mean?"

"I mean you don't just ask to come here to watch me make soap."

"I...I mean...I'm sorry, I didn't mean to presume—"

"You don't get to *watch* me make soap because you have to *help* me make soap. It's no fun if I have to do it all and you only observe." And this could be very fun if it included Jade.

Jade's laugh rang through the phone. "Of course I'll help. You'll have to tell me what to do, because I have no idea."

"I'll tell you what to do, all right." Delany knew how that sounded and made no apologies for it.

"Hey. Behave."

Delany smiled. "This is me behaving. What day were you thinking?"

"When were you thinking of making soap?"

"How about this Saturday?"

"Works for me. Should we let Abby know and see if she wants to join us?"

Delany's spirits dropped a notch. She silently scolded herself. Of course Jade would want Abby to join them. It was only natural.

"Um, sure. I can ask her if you want."

"Great."

They talked for several more minutes before Jade had to get back to work and said goodbye.

Delany put her elbows on the desk and rested her chin on her hands. A few minutes ago she was ready to call Valerie for an appointment and now she wasn't so sure she should do that. Maybe it was better if she let this whole thing drop, to concentrate on her life and her feelings *now* as opposed to some past life that was long gone and couldn't be changed anyway. She sat like that for a long while, squinting her eyes as if that would help her make a better decision. She went back and forth, reasoning with herself, trying to talk herself out of it—unsure what to do. Finally, she dialed the number and explained the situation to Valerie.

"It's not that I don't want to help," Valerie said. "But I know the information from your regression, and I'm afraid that I would be coming into this with a preconceived notion about things. I couldn't give you an unbiased reading, if that makes any sense."

It did, and Delany thanked her for her honesty. She asked Valerie if she could recommend anyone else and wrote down the name and number she gave her.

Another quick phone call and Delany had an appointment on Thursday, two days away, with Sandra Townsend, psychic extraordinaire. At least she hoped she was.

CHAPTER SIXTEEN

Delany pressed the elevator button for the seventh floor. She tried to formulate the questions for the psychic. Should she tell her she wanted to know more about a past life as a young woman named Isobel? Should she tell her the information she already had and ask her to fill in the blanks? Maybe she should ask if she could tell her when Isobel died. Maybe that's why the visions stopped. Maybe Isobel died after receiving the note from Heather. Delany hoped that wasn't the case.

The elevator doors opened and Delany went in search of room 709. The sign on the door said:

Please Don't Knock.
If you have an appointment, please wait
and I'll be with you shortly.
I know you're here.

Delany was a few minutes early. She was too restless to sit, so she leaned back against the wall in an effort not to pace. She had barely settled herself when the door opened and an elderly woman with salt-and-pepper hair tightly pulled back into a ponytail opened the door. She pushed a pair of round wire-rimmed glasses farther up on her nose. "You must be Delany. Pleasure to meet you. I'm Sandra." Delany shook the hand she extended. "Come in, please."

Her office was a single room, painted beige with two tall windows. The usual paraphernalia adorned the shelves on the wall and the table in the corner. Various gemstones—rose quartz, amethyst, and citrine—were sprinkled around the room. The flames from several small candles on the table danced as if in rhythm to the music quietly playing in the background.

Delany started to speak but Sandra put her finger to her lips. "Shh. I don't want you to tell me anything yet. Sit."

Delany did as she was told. Sandra sat across from her.

"I believe I'm here to help you plot out your spiritual life. And spiritual to me means connecting to a higher power. We all come from the same place. It doesn't matter what your name is for that power—God, the Universe, the Creator, Source. I connect to that part of you—to your soul. Others may step in, spirit guides, people that have crossed over, angels—all sorts. I meditated on you before your arrival." She leaned forward. "Is it okay if I take your hands for a few moments?"

Delany nodded, intrigued and hopeful.

Heat radiated from Sandra's hands. She closed her eyes and tilted her head upward as if listening to a voice coming from somewhere else.

Sandra dropped Delany's hands and opened her eyes. "You have been going through so much lately," she said.

Delany nodded. So far so good, but Delany reasoned that most people who visited a psychic did so when life got overwhelming.

"You have someone here with you. She feels like a grandmother to me. Did your grandmother pass?"

Delany nodded again.

"She has a gift for you. She is giving you a jade, and says you will have another coming to you."

Delany's eyes opened wider and her heart pumped harder. A jade? Was it a coincidence, or was her grandmother trying to tell her she would have Jade?

"When our loved ones in spirit give us a gift like that, there is usually a meaning attached. Symbolic. She is giving you her blessing. Jade is said to bless whatever it touches. You should have jade in your life and in your surroundings whenever you can."

I would really like to do that, Delany thought, picturing Jade in her mind.

"You are an old soul. You've been here before. But I feel like you know that. You were created by an energy most call God. You are part of that energy. Everything is connected. Everything is one."

That made sense to Delany. That summed up her belief system pretty well. That gave her confidence that what Sandra was telling her was true.

"You feel like something is slipping away."

Delany opened her mouth to say something and closed it again. *Don't feed the psychic*, Abby had told her. *Let them give you the information. Not the other way around.*

"You have a question. You can ask." Sandra nodded.

Questions, on the other hand, should be okay. "This may sound strange…"

"Honey, there's nothing considered strange in here. Go ahead with your question."

"I've had visions recently of a past life I believe I've had. I had a regression that confirmed it, but lately the visions have stopped and I'm wondering why, and how I can get them back. I want to learn more about that life."

"Is there someone in *this* life that was part of *that* life?"

Delany didn't know if she was asking a general question or she was picking something up through her psychic energies. "Yes." She wondered how much to say.

"You can tell me the name. Female. Right?"

Delany nodded. "Her name is Jade Taylor."

"Ah, yes. Jade. Interesting." Sandra closed her eyes and lifted her hands, turning them toward the ceiling. She held this pose for several seconds.

Delany was sure she wasn't going to get anything. But then

Sandra spoke. "The feeling I'm getting is very volatile in that life. Not necessarily volatile between the two of you, but the people surrounding you. A very dramatic relationship and one in which you were extremely close, like…not sisters…more like best friends. Very, very close. You would have known each other inside and out. I can see little sideways glances, like secrets you would share just by looking at one another. The energies still feel feminine, so I feel like you would have shared that life both being women."

Delany's mouth dropped open at the accuracy. Her heart raced with anticipation.

Sandra continued. "There is a closeness there. Definitely. Unlike anything else you've known in this life."

"Unlike anything I've known with *her* in this life or with *anyone* in this life?"

"With anyone ever in any life. It's very strong and very intimate and I'm sure she feels it as well."

She sure does a great job of hiding it if that's really true. Delany had her doubts about that one. "So, in this lifetime she feels like we had a connection before?"

"I don't think she's accepting of it right now, but through your relationship she will begin to wonder, or at least open up to you that she feels that way. Yes, a very special relationship that was incredibly strong. I'm seeing a marketplace. I feel like you were dark-headed and she was blond, not that it matters much. This lifetime was probably your last before this one, so it's still close and the feelings don't wane much. So knowing one another now would bring it back very strongly.

"I also get a male energy. A jealous one, not happy with you two. Interfering and getting in the way of things."

"Is it possible we were together as lovers in that life?" It was a question that probably didn't need to be asked, because Delany was sure they had been. She just needed Sandra to confirm it.

"That's what it feels like. Your relationship was hidden. Disliked. I feel like this male may have brought it down. I want to say he was a husband of hers, but wait, no…more like a relative or keeper. He did his best to keep you away from her. The two of you had an incredible bond. You have work to finish here."

"So, what can you tell me about *this* life and her?" Delany couldn't help but ask. Sandra seemed so right about everything else. Maybe she could gain some insight into what might happen with Jade.

"There is a block on her part. Probably about accepting feelings for you. I know she has them. She feels strength when she's with you that she hasn't had for a very long time. That's what she loves most about the relationship. Strength and freedom. Does that make sense?"

"I'm not sure. I've only known her a short period of time."

Sandra let out a laugh. "Ah, but you've known her a very long time."

"She's pretty hard to figure out." In fact, she was downright confusing. "Her actions don't match her words, and she isn't very forthcoming."

"She's confused, I think. It's an acceptance on her part, more or less, that needs to happen. That's the impression I get. It feels very secretive from her end, like in the past."

"You mean in the past life?" It was hard for Delany to take everything in. She believed what Sandra said about the past life with Jade but wasn't sure about what she was saying about Jade's feelings now.

"Yes, but it's carried over into this life. She isn't forthcoming now because of what happened in that life."

"Because we had to keep everything a secret then?" Delany wanted to make sure she understood.

"Partly, yes. There was a great betrayal of some kind in that life. It makes her hold back now."

Tears sprang to Delany's eyes. "Did I betray her?" She braced herself for the answer.

"I don't know what the betrayal was. But it was powerful enough to have carried over to the present."

Maybe Irving betrayed her when he forced her to marry. Delany's mind reached for ideas. She knew Isobel loved Heather with all that she was. Delany didn't think she would have betrayed her. But she just didn't know for sure.

Delany wiped a tear from her cheek. "Can you tell me anything else about that life? Can you tell me if we ended up together? Anything at all?"

Sandra shook her head. "I'm not getting anything else."

The answer was within her grasp but had disappeared as she tried to wrap her fingers around it. "How can I get the visions back?" She had to know what happened.

"I'm not sure you can."

Disappointment slammed into Delany's chest. Her voice caught in her throat. "There isn't *any* way?"

"You need to be open. Do you meditate?"

"I haven't in a while. I can definitely start again if you think it will help." She was willing to do anything.

Sandra took Delany's hand. "It certainly couldn't hurt. It quiets the mind. Start with a relaxation technique and let the Universe know you're open to receiving. Ask your spirit guides for help as well. Do you know how?"

"I can do that. You can't get anything else?"

Sandra closed her eyes and took a deep breath. "I'm sorry, honey. That's all the spirits want to share with me today. I hope what I did tell you helps in some way."

Meditate. Delany could do that. Hopefully it would help open the door to the past—a past Delany was anxious to revisit.

CHAPTER SEVENTEEN

Delany had meditated at least once a day since her reading with Sandra. She had to admit she had a greater sense of peace about everything, but the visions and dreams still evaded her. She finished unloading the dishwasher and wiped down the kitchen sink. The only thing left to do before Jade's arrival was sweep the floor. She kept her house fairly neat anyway but wanted to make sure everything was in perfect order today.

You're being an idiot, she told herself as she tucked the broom back into the hall closet. *Jade isn't going to care if your house is spotless or not. It's not going to make her more interested in you.*

"Ha," she said out loud. "It's done now. So whether it makes Jade like me more or not doesn't much matter."

She hesitated about getting her soap-making supplies out yet. That might make the kitchen look untidy and cluttered. She reprimanded herself again and got the supplies from the closet.

She was in the process of rearranging fragrance bottles on the counter, putting them neatly into a line, when the doorbell rang. A pang of nervous excitement hit her in the stomach. She quickly moved a few items around to make them look more organized and went to the door.

She welcomed Jade with a hug, careful not to hold on too long—like she wanted to do.

❖

Jade almost turned back twice before she arrived at Delany's house. When she stopped at the service center on the Thruway it wasn't to get gas or something to eat. It was so she could decide for sure if she wanted to continue and see Delany. It wasn't that she wasn't sure if she wanted to see her. She did. It was actually *because* she wanted to see her so much that she almost turned around and went home. It made no sense. She liked Delany. Liked being with her. But sometimes it seemed overwhelming, almost scary. It was confusing.

Now that she was here she was glad she'd decided to come. She broke into a smile when Delany opened the door. The anxiety she'd felt on the drive over melted away when Delany said, "Hello."

Standing in the kitchen now, shoulder to shoulder with Delany, felt good. Right. It also smelled good. She sniffed the bottle cap Delany held under her nose. "Ooh. I love that one."

"Dragon's blood."

"Is it a blend?"

"Or is it pure dragon's blood, you mean?" Delany said, with a laugh.

Jade bumped her shoulder. "Ha ha. I know it's not really the blood of a dragon. Even an idiot knows that dragons have green blood and that it smells horrid."

"True. This isn't made from real dragons. It does, however, really contain dragon's blood. It's the resin from a plant. It has some other oils mixed in. It's going to turn the soap dark brown when it's cured because it has vanilla, too." She lifted the cap to her nose and breathed in. "It's one of my favorites."

"That doesn't make sense. Vanilla is white."

Delany smiled. "No. Think about it. Vanilla ice cream is white, but pure vanilla is brown. The oil is actually clear, but due to the magic of science we are going to have creamy brown bars of soap when we're done. We'll add a little color to the top to make it more interesting."

"Very cool. Let's use that one for sure," Jade said. "I love vanilla."

"You didn't strike me as a vanilla kind of girl," Delany said. "I thought you were a little spicier than that."

"You're full of it today, aren't you?" She wasn't willing to show Delany just how spicy she could be.

"I'm full of it every day."

They continued opening and smelling the bottles. Delany explained the difference between essential oils and fragrance oils and other tidbits Jade found interesting. She was impressed with Delany's knowledge.

"Okay. We have two choices here. We can make melt-and-pour soap or we can make soap totally from scratch, which is called cold process."

Delany pulled a flat block of white soap out of the box. It was about ten inches on each side and about an inch thick. "This is the melt and pour. We cut it into squares and melt it in the microwave. Once it's melted, we add fragrance and color and pour it into little molds. Quick and easy."

"The soap's already made. That's cheating. How do you make it from scratch?" She peered into the box to see what other goodies it held.

"Basically, we mix lye with water and add it to heated oil. When it's the right consistency we add the fragrance and pour it into a big mold."

"Let's do that one. I want to make real soap from things reason says shouldn't turn into soap, but do."

"Sometimes it's best to throw all reason out the window," Delany said.

Jade suspected she was talking about more than soap. If so, she wasn't willing to go there.

"How do I look?" Jade asked once she was wearing all the paraphernalia Delany insisted she put on. She held up her hands, adorned with bright orange rubber gloves. "My goggles are starting to fog up."

"You still look beautiful. Not many women can rock florescent orange like you can. Here, let me help you with that." Delany put her arms around Jade.

Jade froze, both excited by being so close to Delany and alarmed by it. It took her a few seconds to realize that Delany wasn't embracing her. She was tying the strings that had come undone on the back of the apron she was wearing.

"There, that's better."

Jade breathed a sigh of relief mixed with disappointment when Delany stepped back.

"I'm going to take the water and lye outside to mix," Delany said. "You have to be careful not to breathe it in. Lye can be very dangerous. How about you measure out the coconut and olive oils and add them to the pot on the stove. We need fifteen ounces of each. Think you can figure out the scale?"

"Yep," Jade replied. "Hey, if lye is caustic, how come the soap isn't caustic when it's done?"

"Aww, that's the interesting part. It's called saponification."

"Saponifa...what?"

"Saponification. It's a chemical reaction."

Much like the chemical reaction I have when I'm near you. Jade silently scolded herself for the thought.

"There won't actually be any lye left in the soap when it's done."

"All righty then."

"I'll be back in in a few."

Jade had a sudden urge to kiss her goodbye. "I'll wait here," she said instead.

The oil was in the pot ready to go when Delany returned.

"Now we heat the oil to about a hundred and twenty degrees. You get to stir." She handed Jade a heavy wooden spoon.

❖

They spent the rest of the afternoon making soap, talking and laughing. A lot. Delany was really enjoying herself. Making soap was usually a solitary endeavor. It was nice having company, especially Jade's company.

"When will it be ready to use?" Jade asked.

"It needs to cure for at least four weeks."

"What?"

Delany couldn't help but laugh at the disappointed face Jade made. "It can come out of the mold tomorrow if it's hard enough. I'll slice it into bars, but it has to sit on drying racks before it gets used. You can spend the night if you want to and be here tomorrow to help me unmold and slice it." She held her hands up in the air. "No strings attached." She didn't expect Jade to say yes and was both surprised and thrilled when she did. Delany had trouble containing her smile.

When the last of the mixture was poured, Delany covered the mold and showed Jade how to wrap it in a thick towel to keep the heat in while the magic of saponification happened.

They cleaned the kitchen, washed up, and went out to dinner. Delany had asked Abby to join them, but she had other plans, so Delany got Jade all to herself. It was a little before ten o'clock when they returned home.

Jade declined the glass of wine Delany offered her and Delany wondered if it was because the last time they drank wine together they ended up kissing. That is, until Jade went running off, cutting their evening short.

"I had fun today," Jade said. "Thanks for letting me crash your weekend."

"It was my pleasure. Really. I had a great time, too—I'm *having* a great time."

Jade yawned. "Oh sorry," she said, covering her mouth. "It's not the company."

"Are you tired? The bed in the guest room has clean sheets. It's all ready for you anytime you are." Delany would have liked

Jade to decline the guest room offer and spend the night with her, but she knew it wouldn't happen.

"Thank you. Would you mind terribly if I went to bed?"

Delany consciously hid her disappointment. "Not at all. I'll go up with you and give you something to sleep in." Without her consent, Delany's mind went to an image of Jade naked in her bed. It caused a stir in her stomach and lower. She followed Jade up the stairs, doing her best to keep from staring at her ass, or worse yet, reaching out and touching it.

❖

Jade thanked Delany for use of the T-shirt and sweatpants and closed the door. She knew she had to get herself out of the same room with Delany before something happened. Alcohol would have only made her desire for Delany worse and lowered her ability to control herself. Now, here alone in the room, she knew she'd made the right choice to turn it down. When she'd agreed to spend the night she didn't think it would be a problem, but spending more time with Delany made Jade feel closer to her. Feeling closer made her want more. *More* would not have been a good idea. She only had to think of her ex to know that relationships weren't worth the eventual heartbreak. She instinctually knew that real love wasn't in her future, the same way it hadn't been in her past. Sleeping with Delany would only lead her on and cause pain in the end. She didn't want to cause pain. Somehow, she knew what that pain would look like in Delany's eyes, and the thought of it made her sick to her stomach. But more than that, it made her sad.

She changed out of her clothes and into Delany's. It somehow made Jade feel closer to her. She brought the shirt up to her nose and breathed in, hoping it would smell like Delany. It smelled fresh and recently laundered.

"You're an ass," she whispered to herself. *What's wrong*

with you? Either you want to be with her or you don't. Stop this game in your head. But she couldn't. She crawled into bed and closed her eyes.

Sounds from downstairs told her Delany was still up. Why wouldn't she be? It was still early. Jade would still be up, too, if she were home. But she was here, in this room, hiding out. Hiding from Delany. Or hiding from herself—she wasn't sure which.

❖

Isobel searches her mind for someone who can read Heather's note and can be trusted not to tell anyone about it. Maura. If she's Heather's friend, there's a good chance her family is wealthy and she was taught to read.

"Tomas," she yells to her brother. He's a distance away flirting with Kenna Boyd, the girl he's sweet on. "Tomas," she yells again, running toward him.

"What is it, lass?" he asks, sounding both alarmed and annoyed.

"You need to watch the cart. I have to go find someone." She can barely get the words out, let alone breathe.

He takes her arm and leans in close. "Do not go running after Heather. I have warned you of the trouble that would cause."

"I am not. I promise. I shan't be long. Please."

Tomas turns to Kenna. "I must take my leave but will return before long."

She blushes and nods, and a shy smile graces her face.

Isobel is off and running after Maura before Tomas even reaches their selling cart. She scans the crowd as she weaves in and out of people. It has thinned considerably since the afternoon rush. When she gets to the end of the vendors, she circles back and continues her search in the opposite direction. She starts to give up hope when she spots Maura talking to a boy of similar age.

Isobel slows as she approaches her. She must get her alone. "Excuse me, miss," she says. "May I have a word with you?"

Maura glances around as if she doesn't want anyone to see her talking to Isobel. "I will catch up with you," she says to her companion. "Be quick," she says to Isobel.

"Can you read?"

"What? Why are you asking me such a thing?"

Isobel pulls the folded note from the waistband of her apron and holds it up. "Because I do not know what is written here."

"Let us be away from here," Maura says. "I would be in much trouble if word gets back to Heather's brother that I have helped you. Walk several paces behind me, not too close."

Isobel nods. She waits for Maura to get well ahead of her before following. Maura ducks behind a building and is waiting there when Isobel arrives. She takes the note from Isobel's hand and unfolds it without care.

Isobel waits. Her heart beats so strong in her chest that she is sure Maura must be able to hear it.

"It says—'meet me at the home of your parents fourteen sunrises from today, Heather.'" She hands the note back to Isobel. "I must go now."

"Please tell. Is Heather well? Has any harm come to her?"

"If any harm comes to her, you may well blame yourself. What you have done is sinful. I only bring you this note at Heather's request because I count her a friend. But you are no friend of mine. Were it up to me, I would say for you never to see Heather again. But alas, 'tis not. So, off with you. Do not seek my company again." She leaves without another word.

Isobel stares down at the letter in her hand. Fourteen sunrises. Isobel will count the sunrises until she can see Heather and hold her safe and warm in her arms. Fourteen sunrises. So far away, and yet not as far as forever would be. That is what Isobel thought would pass before she could see Heather again: forever.

With a great deal of care, she folds the thick paper and tucks *it into her apron again. She hurries back to Tomas, her heart alive again with the thought of seeing her love once more.*

Delany woke with a smile on her face. Jade was sleeping in the next room, and she had dreamed of Isobel. And Isobel had plans to meet Heather. It seemed like it might work out for those two after all. She wondered if the sudden return of her visions had anything to do with seeing Jade again. She suspected it might. Glad both for the return of them and for having the opportunity to spend another day with Jade, she slipped out of bed.

Stopping at the guest room, she listened at the door for signs that Jade was awake before taking a quick shower and heading downstairs. The smell of coffee and bacon greeted her.

She found Jade standing at the stove, a coffee cup in one hand and tongs in the other, her back to Delany. Delany watched her for several moments without saying anything. She was about to open her mouth when Jade turned around.

Jade's coffee splashed from the cup as she jumped back. "Oh my God, you startled me." Her hand went to her heart.

Delany tried to hold back her laugh, but some of it slipped through anyway. "I'm so sorry."

Jade shook her head but smiled. "Yeah, I can tell how sorry you are by your giggle."

Delany pulled a sheet of paper towel from the roll and wiped up coffee from the floor. She peered up at Jade. "I honestly didn't mean to do that. I thought you would still be sleeping."

"And I thought I would surprise you with breakfast. Sorry about my coffee."

Delany tossed the paper towel in the trash can under the sink. "No worries. It was my fault."

"You're an early riser," Jade said.

"Always have been. Sometimes I get up before the sun. There can be magic in a sunrise." Fourteen sunrises, to be exact. She tucked Isobel's memories aside and concentrated on starting her day with Jade.

After breakfast Delany let Jade uncover the soap. Jade seemed amazed that the strange mixture of ingredients actually yielded real soap. Delany showed her how to cut it into bars and watched as Jade did it with slow determination. Each bar cut to perfection. Together they laid them across the screens to dry. Jade said she would be back when the soap was ready to use and wouldn't wash her hands until then, so they would be good and dirty. Delany laughed until tears ran down her cheeks.

Isobel hears nothing of Heather in the days that follow. She carefully counts each sunrise to be sure she's at the cabin on the fourteenth day. She marks a tree branch to keep track. Each day she misses Heather more and can hardly wait to see her again. Heather will be here tomorrow and Isobel can't sleep. It's hours before she drifts off, only to awaken when the sun is full in the sky. She leaps out of bed, dresses in a rush, and heads out the door.

"Where are you off to so early?" Tomas's presence just outside the door startles her.

She stumbles over her words. "I—um…I—need some—some time alone. I shall be back later."

"You've yet to even eat this morn."

"I am not hungry. I shall eat when I return." She doesn't wait for Tomas to answer before she's off and running.

Heather is nowhere in sight as Isobel approaches the house. She throws open the door. "Heather?" she says, but hears nothing in return. "Heather?" she says again. Isobel's eyes take a few moments to adjust to the darkness of the room. No one is here.

Maybe she's missed her. Perhaps Heather had arrived and is already gone. Surely she wouldn't leave without somehow letting Isobel know that she'd been here. Isobel looks around for signs of Heather. She sees none. The thin layer of dust on the floor proves no one has been here in days.

Isobel steps outside and closes the door. She leans against it and slides down to the ground. Her mind goes to Heather. She worries for her love's safety. She knows not of the circumstances of Heather's life or how she would be free to meet Isobel. What if Irving caught her trying to leave? What would he do to her? Would he harm or even kill her?

Worry and lack of food turn Isobel's stomach sour. She wishes for water, but there is none nearby. The well has long ago been let to go dry and useless. And she dare not leave to get some.

She sits for a very long time. The sun has risen high in the sky and is on its trek down on the other side of the earth, and still Heather does not arrive. Tomas will be worried about her. But no matter. She'll sit here as long as need be. She'll sit and wait forever.

She dozes off and is awakened some time later by a hand on her shoulder. Heather! But alas, it is not.

"Isobel," Tomas says. "What are you doing?"

"I only want to be alone. Nothing more." She hates lying to him, but knows she must.

"I brought you some food." He hands her a sack and a small jug of water.

She pulls the cork on the jug and lifts it to her lips. The water is warm like the day, but much appreciated. "Thank you," she says, when she's had her fill.

"Eat something," Tomas urges.

Her stomach won't hear of it. "I will in a little while."

Tomas sits down beside her. "Isobel, what is going on with you? You have been sulking for days, and today, you take off without a word. If you had not nearly run over me, I would not have even known you'd left."

Isobel worries Heather will arrive, see Tomas, and leave. She glances over his shoulder. It doesn't escape his notice.

He turns to look in that direction. "Are you waiting for Heather?"

She nods.

"Isobel, I heard she left three days ago to be married. I dared not tell you for fear of your reaction."

She tries to speak, but no words come out. How could that be true? Heather is supposed to meet her here this very day. This very day! The world swims before her as tears pool and fall in streams down her face.

Tomas takes her in his arms and strokes her hair. "There, there, Bellie. So sorry. I know she was your friend. I know you shall miss her. Maybe someday you shall see her again."

Isobel pushes out of his arms. She doesn't want his comfort, for there is no comfort for her now. She rises. "I want to be alone, Tomas. Please let me be."

She's sorry for the hurt in his eyes but has nothing left in her that can make it better. He'll get over his hurt. She knows she never will. "Tomas, please," she says again, and walks away from the house, through the trees.

"Isobel," he calls after her. "Isobel, I shall let you be, but you must promise to come home soon, by nightfall at least."

Without turning around she raises a hand to signal she's heard him. She knows he's standing there watching her and will do so until well past the time she's out of sight.

"Isobel," she hears, from somewhere off to the side of her.

She turns her head in the direction of the voice. Heather stands behind a tree, finger to her lips. "Shh," she says. "Do not say anything. Tomas mustn't know I'm here."

CHAPTER EIGHTEEN

Delany set her camera down on the weatherworn bench beside her. Taking pictures of the ducks in the lake on this beautiful spring day could wait. This was the third time Jade and Delany had talked on the phone since spending their soap-making weekend together, less than a week ago. Delany was starting to wonder if Jade might, in fact, have feelings for her like the psychic predicted. Maybe Jade wasn't even acknowledging those feelings to herself. Even if that *was* the case, Delany wasn't going to push. If Jade wanted more than friendship, she was going to have to be the one to make the first move. Delany was careful not to show too much interest.

"I'm glad you called," Delany said, pushing any excitement from her voice.

"I'm calling to check on the soap."

Delany laughed. "Wait. I'll let you talk to it, then."

"Funny. I want to talk to you."

"Good to know. It's getting there. I turned them today to make sure they dry evenly. They're darkening up nicely."

"I'm glad you let me help. I had a really nice time."

Delany smiled at the memory. "Me too. Have you washed your hands since you went home?"

"Nope."

Delany could tell she was smiling. "Not even after you've gone to the bathroom?"

"A lady never tells."

"A lady washes her hands after she goes to the bathroom." Delany liked the sound of Jade's laugh.

"True that."

"So, when am I going to get to see you again?" Delany tried to stop the words from coming out of her mouth, but they poured out anyway.

If Jade minded the question, she didn't let on. "Oh, I don't know. Maybe I'll surprise you one of these days."

Delany was astonished by her answer. "Surprises can be nice."

Isobel gasps at how tired and worn Heather looks. Her dress, ripped and dirty, lies limp across her slumped shoulders. Bloodied scratches on her face and arms are starting to scab over. "Go back and tell Tomas you are all right and will be home soon," she says. "Get him to leave. I shall wait here."

Isobel does as Heather has instructed. It takes a little convincing, but she finally gets him to leave. She turns and walks back to the tree where Heather was hiding. She is no longer there. Isobel wonders if she has run off or, even worse, she has imagined her.

"Heather," she says. Her heart pounds as she waits for an answer.

She hears the sound of twigs breaking and sees Heather step out from behind a different tree. She wants to rush to her, to hold her. But she stares instead, unable to move, afraid that if she reaches out and touches her, she won't be real.

"Isobel." Heather puts her arms out and Isobel steps into them. She is wrapped in love and held close. She trembles as relief sweeps over her. They stay like this for a long time, each afraid to let go of the other. Finally, Isobel takes Heather's hand and leads her to the house, retrieving the water that Tomas left.

Isobel sits Heather down on the edge of the bed. "Oh, my love. Pray tell, what has happened?" She doesn't wait for the answer before asking more questions. "Are you all right? You are hurt. Did Irving do this to you?" Pouring water on the hem of her dress, Isobel gently wipes away some of the dirt and blood from Heather's face. She carefully sweeps the material over her cheeks, her chin, her forehead, and finally her lips. The breath she lets out has been trapped within her for weeks. "Heather?" She looks into her eyes, waiting for answers.

"Shh. There is time for that."

Time for that. They had time now. Time to be together... forever, Isobel dared believe.

"I promise to explain it all. I need to rest. I have been walking for days."

"Oh, my dear sweet Heather." She hands Heather the jug and encourages her to drink. Explanations can wait. Right now it is only important that Heather is here and that she is safe. Isobel kisses Heather on the forehead and gently lays her back on the bed. She crawls in next to her and wraps her in her arms. They lie together, Isobel listening to the rhythm of Heather's breathing until it changes and she knows she's asleep. In the morn, she is sure Heather will tell her of the harrowing tale that has brought them back together.

CHAPTER NINETEEN

Jade planned on driving to Rochester today and surprising Delany. An appearance at her parent's house and letting Abby know she was coming were also on her agenda. Maybe Abby would join Delany and her for dinner. Actually, she wasn't even sure she was having dinner with Delany. She was hoping, but considering she hadn't told Delany she was coming, she had no idea if she would be free.

She reformulated the plan in her head. She wouldn't tell anyone she was coming for a visit. She would go to Delany's house first, and if Delany was home and available, she would spend the day with her. They could decide together if they should ask Abby to join them. If Delany wasn't home, or had other plans, Jade would go visit Abby and then her parents. It sounded good in theory. She hoped it worked out in reality.

She showered and dressed, humming to herself the whole time. She was in a good mood, for sure. It was more than it just being a Saturday and her day off. She'd had plenty of those. Today she would have someone other than Cliché to keep her company. She was hoping that someone would be Delany.

❖

Delany went to the door wondering who could be ringing the bell on a Saturday morning. She wasn't expecting company.

She was surprised and pleased to see her sister standing there. "Hi, Mary," Delany said. "Where's the munchkin?"

"Lizzy has a playdate. I've got a whole hour before I have to go pick her up. I thought I would surprise you with breakfast." She held up a bag from McDonald's and a cardboard tray holding two paper cups of coffee.

Delany stepped back to let her pass, grabbing one of the cups.

"I wanted to celebrate your Scottish past life with food from McDonald's. That's a Scottish name, isn't it? Or is it Irish?"

Delany laughed. "I'm pretty sure that whatever is in that bag doesn't resemble any kind of ethnic food from either of those countries."

"Are you positive? I'm pretty sure the Egg McMuffin was invented in Scotland. Taste it and see if it reminds you of home."

"Sit your ass down and stop making fun of me," Delany said good-naturedly. She pulled out a chair at the kitchen table for her sister.

"Sorry. I'm just teasing you."

Delany sat down on the opposite side of the table. "I know. I must make it pretty easy with all my crazy talk."

"Anything new going on with that?"

Delany filled Mary in on the latest visions. "I don't know where it's going, but I'm super interested in finding out."

"Don't the visions interfere with your daily life?"

Delany unwrapped her breakfast sandwich and took a bite before answering. She shook her head. "Not really. I think about them a lot, but they don't interfere. A lot of them come as dreams."

"How do you know that's not all they are—just normal dreams?"

Delany had considered this question herself. "Well, first of all, they feel different. They aren't bits and pieces. They're sequential and make perfect sense. Dreams make sense when you're dreaming them, but when you wake up, you realize that most dreams wouldn't happen in real life, like you can fly, or you're out in public in your pajamas. Dreams also fade as the day goes on. These don't. They're very clear and very real in my mind. If I—or should I say Isobel—touches something, I can feel it. I can actually feel its texture. I can feel how soft Heather's lips are."

"And you still haven't told Jade any of this?" Mary went to the freezer, retrieved a couple of ice cubes, and added them to her coffee.

"I've come close a couple of times. I don't think I'll ever be able to." She just didn't trust that Jade would understand. And there was really no reason to tell her, other than the occasional feeling that she was lying by omission.

"I'm sorry, Delany. I know you wish you could."

"I do. But don't think it would go well. It's not your normal topic of conversation."

"Very true. What does Abby say about all this?"

"She's worried that I'll get my heart broken. She hasn't said as much, but I think she would prefer it if I let it all drop."

"And you don't want to do that?" Mary took a bite of her hash browns.

"No way. I truly feel like I need to know what happened." It was more than a need. It was a mission at this point.

"But it doesn't really make any difference now what happened then, does it?"

"I can't answer that. I think some of the feelings, both the good ones and the hard ones, have carried through to this life." Delany not only believed what the psychic had told her about this, she felt it as well.

"So, what do you do with that?"

"I wish I knew."

❖

Seeing Delany's car in the driveway was a good sign. Seeing the car parked behind it, however, was not. It hadn't occurred

JOY ARGENTO

to Jade that if Delany was home, she might not be alone. She wondered if Delany would tell her if she was dating anyone. They talked about a lot of things on the phone, but the subject of dating never came up.

Jade pulled in next to the car and wondered if she should park and go to the door or back up and leave. She didn't like the lump that was forming in her throat or the sick feeling in her stomach—a feeling she had no right to be feeling. Delany was a free agent. A beautiful woman. If she wanted to see someone, she certainly had that right. She deserved to be dating someone. She deserved to be happy. And who wouldn't want to be with her? *I'm sure plenty of women want to date her.* The thought wasn't comforting.

Jade was still sitting in her car when the front door of Delany's house opened. If she left now, whoever had opened the door would see her leaving. She had no choice but to stay.

A beautiful woman with blond shoulder-length hair emerged from the house. She turned and gave Delany a hug. Her slender hips swayed as she walked to her car. She gave Jade a wide smile and a nod of her head, her eyes bright with excitement.

Jade didn't know what the hell to think. If this woman was Delany's overnight date, she gave no indication that Jade being there was a problem. The woman turned and waved at Delany. Delany waved back and then waved at Jade.

Jade felt like she had been caught spying. She waited for the woman to back out of the driveway before getting out and walking toward the house. The smile on Delany's face was unmistakable, but Jade didn't know if it was for her or for the woman who had just left. She resisted the urge to ask.

"Hi there. What a great surprise." Delany pulled her into a tight hug.

Jade felt her body melt into Delany's but stopped herself from sinking too far into the sensation. "Hope I didn't interrupt anything," Jade said, steeling herself for the answer.

"Nothing to worry about. Come on in."

Jade didn't know what to make of that answer. It was neither reassuring nor incriminating. Not that it would be incriminating if Delany had spent the night with someone. Jade told herself that she had no right to the feeling of disappointment at the thought.

"I'll make us some coffee," Delany said, once they were inside. She led the way to the kitchen and popped a pod into her Keurig. "Cream, no sugar. Right?"

Jade smiled and nodded. She liked that Delany had remembered. She remembered a lot of small things like that.

"Come, sit out on the deck with me," Delany said, handing her the mug of steaming coffee. "It's such a beautiful day."

Jade followed her out the sliding glass door and sat in a wide wicker chair.

"I thought if you didn't have plans, we might spend the day together." Jade held her breath waiting for Delany's response.

Delany sat down across from her. "Nothing I can't rearrange. I would love to spend the day with you."

Relief washed over Jade like a wave. It surprised her how much she had wanted Delany to be free for the day. "We can even ask Abby if she would like to join us for dinner, if you want." Before she could stop herself she added, "And your friend who was leaving when I got here. Who was that?" She averted her eyes. *Oh shit. Didn't mean to ask that.*

"That blond beauty was my sister. She got all the looks in the family, but luckily I got all the brains. I would have introduced you if she hadn't been in such a hurry to pick up her daughter."

Jade couldn't stop the smile that spread across her face. So it wasn't a date after all. "I'd like to meet her sometime. And it's good that you got all the brains, because beauty fades."

"I know. Right?" Her face lit up.

Jade's heart warmed to it. *Your sister's got nothing on you when it comes to beauty.* "We can invite her to dinner, too. It would be great to get to know your family."

"That's sweet. I know she's got plans tonight, but I'm sure we can do it another time. I do think we should ask Abby, though. I know she would love to catch up with you. Does Abby know you're here? In town, I mean."

"No. I didn't tell anyone. Took the chance you'd be free."

"How about your parents? Are you planning on seeing them while you're here?"

"Shh." Jade put her finger to her lips. "I won't tell them I'm in town if you don't."

Delany laughed. "I don't know if I should be flattered because you came to see me and are ignoring them or feel guilty because I'm keeping you from them."

Jade held her hands face up as if they were a scale and she was weighing the words. "Flattered," she said, lowering her left hand. "Or guilty…" She lowered the right hand. "I definitely think you should feel flattered. Guilt is such a wasted emotion."

Delany smiled over the edge of her coffee cup. "Okay. Flattered it is. I'm so glad you're here."

"Truth be told, I only came because I figure the soap we made would be ready to use." She did her best not to laugh.

"Oh, is that so? So, it's really only the soap you came to see?"

"Don't be silly. I'm glad you're here, too. How else would I have gotten in if you weren't here to open the door?" she teased.

To her surprise, Delany put her coffee cup down, got up, and offered Jade her hand. "Come on then. Let's go check it out. It's still on the racks."

Jade took the hand Delany offered, trying to ignore the softness and warmth of it, and followed Delany inside. The scent of dragon's blood met her in the doorway of the laundry room where the soap was drying.

"Can I touch it?" she asked, picking up a bar before waiting for an answer. It was much harder and a darker brown than it had been the day they cut it and set it out to dry.

Delany smiled at her. "You're like a kid in a candy store."

She smiled back. "This is so cool. We made real soap. It really spontifi-whatever-you-call-it."

"Want to try it?" Delany asked her.

Sure. How about I wash your back—and maybe your front—in the shower, she thought. "Of course," she said to Delany. *Knock that shit off*, she said to her brain.

CHAPTER TWENTY

*T*he sun is starting to set when Isobel feels Heather stir in her arms.

"You must go home before Tomas comes to find you," Heather tells her. *"You mustn't tell him I'm here. And please do not feel guilty. Guilt is such a wasted emotion."*

"I'll not tell. But I do not want to leave you." Isobel is afraid if she leaves, Heather might not be here when she returns.

Heather is quick to reassure her. *"Go home for now. I shall wait here. When your uncle and Tomas are asleep, come back. I shall tell you then what has happened. We can make a plan so we can stay together always."*

Isobel kisses Heather and slips out of bed. *"I shan't be long,"* she tells her. *"Please, for the sake of all that is holy, stay here."* Please.

"I promise. I will await your return."

She slowly walks to the door, afraid to take her eyes off Heather. She lifts the latch to leave.

"Isobel," Heather says. *"I love you."*

"And I, you." Isobel leaves the cabin before she has a chance to change her mind. The cool night air caresses her skin as she makes her way home by the light of the moon.

Tomas is outside waiting for her when she arrives. *"I was worried,"* he says.

"I am sorry. I did not mean to make you worry for me." She hesitates. *"I miss Heather. I fear not seeing her."*

"Dinner is on the table for you. Go eat. Off with you now."

She does as she's told. Her uncle isn't home. He's probably in the village drinking mash with his friends, as he often does. He never checks on her upon his return, so he won't miss her when she sneaks out later, if he hasn't returned home by then. She wonders how long it will be before Tomas lays his head down to sleep.

❖

"That was delicious," Jade said, sliding her plate forward. It had been a wonderful day with Delany and a very nice dinner out. "I'm going to excuse myself to the little girls' room."

"I'll go with you," Abby said, pushing her chair back.

"You seem to be spending a lot of time with Delany," Abby said, when they were alone.

Jade's first impulse was to somehow deny it or lessen the fact that she enjoyed Delany's company. She wasn't sure why she felt the need to do that. Maybe if Abby thought she had feelings for Delany, she would want them together. Jade still didn't think that was a good idea. Abby would want to know why, and Jade didn't have an answer that would appease her. Of course, she didn't really have a reason. Except for the fear that cropped up every time she entertained the thought.

"Yeah. I guess I have." She checked her makeup in the mirror in an attempt to somehow lessen the impact of the conversation.

"I don't want to see either one of you get hurt, Jade."

She turned toward Abby. "What does that mean?"

"Don't lead her on."

"What the hell, Abby? I'm not leading her on. She's a big girl. She can decide if she wants to hang out with me or not."

"We both know she has feelings for you. I just want to make

sure you're not playing with them." The stern look on Abby's face told Jade just how serious she was.

"I've been honest with her about not wanting a relationship. She's willing to be my friend." Jade was consciously trying to keep the annoyance out of her voice. She was having a hard enough time trying to sort through her own feelings without Abby sticking her nose in the middle of it. "I thought you were my friend, too."

Abby's tone softened and she touched Jade's arm. "Of course I'm your friend. I'm sorry. I'm worried about Delany. I know you would never do anything to purposely hurt her."

"I wouldn't. I do care about her and I like spending time with her." Was that all she felt? She knew it wasn't. But friendship was all she was willing to offer Delany. Wasn't it?

"Just be careful. Okay?"

"I will," Jade promised. The last thing she would ever want to do was hurt Delany.

Abby gave her a hug. "I'm sorry. I worry—about both of you."

❖

Isobel stands at the door. Her heart beats wildly in her chest with the knowledge that Heather is inside. She pulls up the latch and enters to find Heather asleep on the bed. Taking great pains to be quiet, she starts a fire in the fireplace.

Isobel strips down to her undergarment, leaving her smock in a heap on the floor next to Heather's dress. Gingerly lifting the covers, she slips in beside Heather and wraps her arms around her warm body. The fire casts a warm golden glow about the room and across Heather's sleeping face. Isobel leans in and kisses Heather softly on the lips.

"Hello," Heather says, eyes still closed, voice filled with sleep. She smiles and pulls Isobel in closer.

"Sorry. I tried not to wake you."

"I am glad you did." Heather runs her fingers over Isobel's cheek and across her lips. Slowly. Softly. Tenderly.

"I missed you so."

"And I, you." Heather lays Isobel back fully and kisses her.

A moan escapes from Isobel as Heather's tongue enters her mouth. Her own tongue welcomes it in.

Isobel strokes Heather's arms. Skin, soft beneath her fingertips. She breaks the kiss long enough to whisper, "I love you." And she does. With all her heart and deep in her soul. She has never known love like this before.

"I love you, too. So much."

Isobel's need to touch Heather and to be touched overwhelms her, and her eyes fill with tears. Heather brushes them away and once again pulls her into a kiss.

With trembling fingers, Isobel strokes Heather's breast through the thin material of her slip. A rush of wetness soaks her as Heather sucks in a breath and releases it with a moan. Heather's nipple instantly hardens under Isobel's touch. Isobel wants—no—needs to feel Heather's skin. She pulls down the strap of the slip and glides her hand across Heather's shoulder and under the material. She kneads and caresses the soft full breast. It fits like it was made to be in her hand.

Heather tugs at Isobel's arm. "Wait," she says, and struggles to sit up.

Isobel's heart sinks, fearing she has gone too far. Heather wants her to stop. She shouldn't have touched Heather that way.

Isobel moves back, allowing Heather to sit upright. Isobel is sure she's going to get out of the bed and leave. She opens her mouth to apologize, but Heather hushes her with a finger to the lips. Heather pulls the slip above her head and drops it to the floor.

The beauty of Heather's naked body, golden from the light of the fire, takes Isobel's breath away. She knows she should avert her eyes but can't. She reaches out and strokes first the side of

Heather's breast then the center, sweeping her fingers slowly down, across the nipple. The urge to take it into her mouth, to caress it with her tongue, surprises her. She looks into Heather's eyes for reassurance. For permission. She finds her answer there without Heather uttering a word.

She places a gentle kiss upon the nipple before sucking it hungrily into her mouth. Her tongue dances with delight all around it. Her hand finds its way to the other breast and holds it possessively.

The sounds coming from Heather's throat and the sensations of touching her cause a stirring deep within Isobel that settles squarely in her center. How can touching Heather cause her own body to react so?

Heather pulls at Isobel's undergarment, and Isobel stops long enough to allow its removal. It joins Heather's discarded slip on the floor.

Isobel is not shy about Heather seeing her naked. She sees the want in Heather's eyes as they flicker over her body. She brings them up to Isobel's face, and they sit for what seems like an eternity, staring into each other's eyes. The light from the fire and from their very souls dances there.

Heather moves a stray piece of hair from Isobel's face and hooks her hand behind her neck, bringing Isobel closer. She kisses her with the same passion Isobel feels.

They lower to the bed until they are lying down, the weight of Heather's body on hers. Breasts on top of breasts. Mouths meshed together. Hearts beating as one.

Isobel opens her legs and feels Heather press her nakedness into the wetness there. Her hips rise to meet Heather and they move in unison with a rhythm that speaks in a song that only they can hear.

Heather's hand searches Isobel's body, finding her breasts and claiming them as her own. Her fingers take ownership as they caress and stroke the tender flesh.

Isobel feels heat rising from her belly and spreading to every part of her body. She is on fire with desire, unlike anything she has ever known. She feels the need to have Heather inside her. To feel her fingers caress the walls that make her a woman. She places her hand on top of Heather's and guides her there, to the place of her greatest need.

Without words, Heather understands what she is asking for. Raising her body enough to give her room, she pushes first one finger, then two, into Isobel.

Isobel's moan is matched by Heather's. It only takes several strokes of Heather's fingers inside her for the explosion that she feels coming, yet is unprepared for. It brings a shudder through her body and a sob to her throat.

"Are you all right? Did I hurt you?" Heather asks softly, pushing the hair from Isobel's face and brushing away a tear.

Isobel pulls her in for a deep kiss before answering. She finds it hard to speak, her breath coming in gasps. "You are so beautiful," she says. "You did not hurt me. You made me feel more wonderful than I could have ever imagined possible."

"Oh, Isobel. I do love you so."

"And I, you, my dear sweet Heather."

She plants several gentle kisses on Heather's brow and eyelids. They lie in each other's arms until Isobel's heartbeat slows to a regular rhythm. The light from the fire is fading, but the heat it generates isn't needed because the heat inside Isobel and radiating off Heather's body is enough to keep them warm.

"I need to touch you. To feel you. To make you mine, wholly," Isobel whispers.

"I am wholly yours and only yours."

Isobel wraps her arms around Heather and rolls her onto her back. Now on top, Isobel kisses her. Heather's tongue enters her mouth and she welcomes it in. Her hands wander down Heather's sides, caressing her rib cage, her waist, her hips— soft—so soft. In contrast, Heather's nipple becomes hard, the skin firm when Isobel strokes it.

Heather moans and a surge of wetness fills Isobel at the sound. She wonders how wet Heather's center is. She needs to know. To feel it. She slips down on to her side so her hand has the freedom to explore the area she seeks.

Isobel is delighted by how wet Heather is as she strokes through the tangle of hair and into the folds of Heather's heat. Heather's hips rise to meet Isobel's hand. Isobel wants to push her fingers into Heather, the way Heather did to her, but fear holds her back. She is unsure how to do it. Heather's hand is on top of hers and guides her in.

She feels the moisture and heat as Heather's body closes around her fingers and seems to pull them in. Isobel has no choice but to comply with Heather's request and her own desire to fill Heather, to be as close to her as possible—to join their two bodies as one.

Her mouth leaves Heather's and she kisses a trail down Heather's neck to her chest. She places a lingering kiss in the center and feels Heather's rapid heartbeat with her lips. Heather's sounds urge her on, and she kisses first one breast and then the other, sucking the hard nipple into her mouth. Her tongue sweeps across it, tasting the salty sweetness of Heather's flesh.

She can't get enough of this beautiful woman beside her. Their bodies move in unison. As if Isobel can read Heather's mind and her desires, her mouth leaves Heather's breast and continues the trail of kisses downward until her mouth meets the junction where her fingers are deep inside Heather. She hesitates only a moment before dipping her head and tasting Heather's sweetness.

Heather's moan at the contact is loud, and Isobel pushes her tongue deeper into the folds. Heather's hands on the back of Isobel's head hold her in place, but she needs no encouragement to continue. She has found the center of life here, and nothing can stop her from the want to explore it, to feel it, to taste it, to possess it.

Heather sucks in a deep breath and holds it as a strong ripple runs through her body. She sits halfway up, clutching Isobel's head in her arms, then collapses backward onto the bed.

Chapter Twenty-One

Jade sat down at the table and forced a smile. The exchange with Abby in the bathroom left her more shaken than she realized. Was she leading Delany on only to hurt her in the end? Was she fooling herself? She knew her feelings for Delany grew stronger each time they were together. Maybe continuing to see her wasn't such a good idea. Maybe it was better to cut her losses and stay away from her altogether. But that itself would be a loss. A loss that Jade didn't want. She wanted to keep Delany in her life. She felt good around Delany, somehow stronger. She also felt free to be herself and still be accepted.

She didn't have a lot of people in her life, by choice. She often felt safer alone. But she didn't feel that way around Delany. She felt safe with her. She knew if she offered Delany her heart, Delany would protect it and keep it from harm. But there was still something standing in the way of her doing that, and Jade wasn't quite sure what it was. It was like a pinprick in her heart, a wound that hadn't quite healed—a longing for something from Delany, and at the same time, a fear. It made no sense at all.

"Everything okay?" Delany tapped a finger on the back of her hand.

"Yeah. Why?" Jade looked at her and did her best to smile.

"You look a little flushed is all. Feeling all right?"

"Everything's fine. More than fine. It's great. I'm having a good time." She turned to Abby. "And I'm so glad you could have dinner with us."

"Me too," Abby said.

Jade knew she meant it. They had been friends too long to let a few harsh words come between them. Abby had truly been worried about Delany. And why shouldn't she be? Jade could hurt her if she wasn't careful. So that meant she had to be careful. Or maybe it meant she had to reexamine her own feelings for Delany and come to a different conclusion—maybe think about the possibility of seeing her, as in dating her. Would that even work? They lived an hour and a half away from each other. Other couples did it with relative ease. Other couples. Did she want to try to be a couple with Delany? She smiled to herself at the idea.

The more she got to know Delany, the better she liked her. Liked—was that a strong enough word for her feelings? Was she fooling herself when she said she didn't want a relationship with anyone? Delany wasn't just anyone. She was…well…special.

"What do you think, Jade?" Delany's voice pulled her out of her own head. She realized she hadn't been listening to the conversation.

"Um, what? Sorry. I missed the question."

"I asked you if we should give Abby some of the soap we made."

"I don't know," Jade said, with a smile. "What has she ever done for us?"

"Well"—Delany put her hand over Jade's—"Abby introduced us, and for that I will be eternally grateful. I value your friendship."

The warmth of Delany's hand penetrated Jade's skin and made its way to her heart. *Friendship.* Delany referred to it as friendship. And why wouldn't she? That had been how Jade insisted they keep it. But now she didn't think she liked the limits of that word.

"Should we share the riches?" Delany asked.

"Absolutely. Abby, you're going to love the dragon's blood.

That's my favorite." Against her will, Jade had an image of Delany in the shower with her. She was running her sudsy hands from a bar of the homemade soap over Delany's body. A surge of warmth and moisture rushed through her. She blinked a few times, trying to dislodge the image. What was wrong with her? She was having a nice dinner with friends, which was no time for thoughts like that. But her mind returned to the image and her body followed suit. Delany was talking but Jade wasn't listening. Her eyes focused on Delany's lips, not her words. Lips that she had kissed. Lips that she wanted to kiss now. They were no longer the lips of a stranger. They were Delany's lips, and God help her, Jade wanted to possess them.

Delany didn't know what had transpired between Abby and Jade in the bathroom, but Jade seemed distracted when they returned to the table. It had been quite a surprise to see her in the driveway that morning—a very pleasant surprise. She loved spending time with her, but it was getting harder and harder to remind herself that they were just friends and that might be all they ever would be. She had come to think of Isobel and Heather as separate entities from her and Jade. Their story seemed removed from who they were now. She knew her feelings for Jade were real and current, not some leftover remnants from the past. For now—maybe for always—she would have to be content to enjoy whatever time she did get to spend with her and try not to hope for anything more. But she did hope for more. It was hard not to.

"Do I only get the dragon's blood or do I have more to choose from?" Abby's words dragged Delany back into the conversation.

"Nope. Just the dragon's blood," Delany said.

"Okay. I guess beggars can't be choosers."

Delany laughed. "You are far from a beggar, Abby. You're more like a bag lady that has everything she needs in her shopping cart. A bar of soap would just add to your already full life."

Abby laughed. "I have no idea what that even means. Is it a compliment or an insult?"

"Would I ever insult you?"

"In a heartbeat."

"It was a compliment." Delany paused. "I think."

The waitress took that moment to step up to the table. "Everyone up for dessert tonight?" she asked.

"None for me," Jade said. The other two women followed suit.

"Then I'll just leave this with you," the waitress said, setting down the faux-leather folder containing their bill.

Jade reached for it at the same time Delany did. "This is my treat," Jade said.

"Oh no," Delany answered. "You showing up at my door this morning was a treat. I'll take care of the bill."

"I think not. I've got this."

"Children, children," Abby said, pulling the folder from them. "Stop your quibbling. I'll pay for this and you two play nice." She put her hand up in the air to stop their protests and put her credit card in the small plastic sleeve.

They stayed for only a short while longer once the waitress returned with Abby's credit card and a receipt.

"Shall we?" Delany asked Jade.

They said their goodbyes to Abby in the parking lot and got into Delany's car.

Delany glanced at Jade. The soft glow from the nearby streetlight illuminated her near-perfect profile, and Delany had trouble looking away.

"I'm so glad you were you were free today. It was great spending the day with you."

"I feel the same. I really enjoyed myself. I'm free tomorrow, too," Delany said, hoping Jade would get the hint.

"Oh you are, are you? What did you have in mind?"

"Well, I was hoping you would be spending the night. In the

guest room, of course," Delany added. "And we could go to the art gallery or maybe take in a movie tomorrow. Whatever you want. What do you think?" *Please say yes.*

"You're in luck. I happened to put extra food out for Cliché, who sends his love, by the way, so I am free to spend another day. Are you sure I'm not messing up your plans for the weekend?"

I would gladly change whatever plans I had in favor of spending the day with you, Delany thought but didn't dare say out loud. "You're not messing up anything."

"Okay then. It's a plan."

Delany smiled. She got to spend another day with Jade. At the same time her heart warmed to the thought, her brain yelled out a warning. *The more time you spend with her, the more connected you feel and the more you want her. You're going to get your heart broken.*

I'll take my chances, Delany told her brain. She didn't want to think about that. But she knew all too well the possibility of it happening.

❖

"Wine?" Delany asked, once they were back at her place.

Jade had had two glasses at the restaurant—one more wouldn't hurt. "Sure." She watched Delany head toward the kitchen. She couldn't shake the urge to kiss her. Maybe another glass of wine wasn't the best idea.

I'm a grown-up. I can control myself.

But she couldn't seem to control her thoughts, and the thought of kissing Delany was front and center, crowding all logic out. *No. There will be no kissing. And no more* thoughts *of kissing,* she told her brain.

She started to follow Delany into the kitchen but Delany stopped suddenly and turned, running right into her.

"I'm sor—" she started.

Her words were cut off as Jade, without missing a beat, and much to her own surprise, wrapped her arms around Delany and kissed her full on the mouth.

As suddenly as she'd started the kiss, Jade stopped it. "Oh my God. I am so sorry." Heat emanated from every pore. She backed away from Delany. "I didn't mean to do that." What the hell had come over her?

"It sure felt like you meant it. Please don't apologize. Actually, please don't be sorry you did it. I'm not."

"Oh geez. I shouldn't have—"

"Stop saying that."

"Sor…I…" Jade let out a breath. "Okay. I'm not sorry I did it. I…oh, I don't know what I'm saying." She was light-headed and more than a little turned on.

"That kiss got you all kinds of flustered, huh?"

Jade nodded. She had wanted to kiss Delany all night but hadn't actually planned on doing it. She hadn't expected Delany to stop so suddenly, and when she bumped into her, her body had taken over. Her mind had no say in the matter. And Delany had kissed her back. *Really* kissed her back. She was at a loss as to what to do about it. A part of her wanted nothing more than to sweep Delany off her feet, take her upstairs, and make wild, passionate love to her. Another part of her wanted to run screaming from the room from embarrassment and fear.

Fear.

There it was again.

What the hell?

They were two consenting adults. They could do as they pleased. What was there to be afraid of? Now wasn't the time to figure it out. She realized Delany was staring at her. She had to think of something to say. "Um, I sure could use that glass of wine now." *Smooth. Way to change the subject.*

"Sure. Make yourself comfortable in the living room and I'll bring it in."

Jade did as she was told, relieved for the chance to be alone for a few minutes to collect her thoughts. Okay, so she'd kissed Delany. What was the big deal? The big deal was Delany wanted more, and she knew it. But *she* wanted more, too. Didn't she? So many questions, not enough answers. What exactly did she want from Delany? Right now, she knew she wanted sex. Did she want more than that? Maybe she did. No, no maybe about it. She did. She wanted to explore the possibility of a real relationship with Delany. Delany wanted that, too. Didn't she?

"Here you go," Delany said, handing her a glass of wine. Delany sat in the chair across from her instead of next to her on the couch. "Want to talk about it?"

Jade sipped her wine trying to buy time before answering.

Delany waited.

"I'm not sure there's anything to talk about. I got caught up in a moment and—"

"And what? Is that all there was to it? I mean if that's all it was, we can forget it happened." Delany paused. "If that's what you want."

That's not what I want. She wasn't sure she was willing to say the words out loud. She sipped her wine again.

"So, I guess that's what you want. Okay. We'll pretend it never happened. So how about those Yankees?" Delany smiled.

That was one of the things Jade loved about her. Her smile. Wait. What? Loved? Did Jade love her? Was that possible? Her head started to swim with all the thoughts rushing through it. *Okay, one thing at a time. Address Delany's question. Be honest, but don't give too much away until you figure this out.* "I, um…I mean, um…well…"

Delany raised her eyebrows.

"Let's try this again," Jade said, determined to explain. "I don't know for sure what I want or what I'm feeling at the moment. I wish I could be clearer, but that's the best I can do." Oh, how she wished she could put on her sneakers and go for a run. Her feet pounding the pavement, moving as fast as her legs could carry her. It would help clear her head.

"Well, okay then. You take all the time you need to figure this out. I'm hoping you will let me know when you do," Delany said, with complete sincerity.

Yeah. I'm falling for her. What am I going to do about it? She had no idea.

"Want to watch a movie?" Delany asked, trying to break the tension, Jade suspected.

"Sure."

Delany listed off some movie titles. "Or we can see what's on Netflix."

Jade realized she hadn't been listening, still in her own head. "How about we see what's on Netflix?"

Delany turned on the TV and scrolled through the list of movies.

"How about that one?" Jade asked.

"That's one of the ones I said I have." Delany laughed. "You weren't even paying attention, were you?"

"Was too," Jade said, with a childish whine.

"Were not," Delany mimicked back.

Jade relaxed, not sure it if was the playful banter or the wine. Whatever it was, she was glad for it. "Anything you want to watch is fine."

"We'll watch this one. And we'll watch it on Netflix instead of my DVD because that's what you picked."

"Smart-ass," Jade said.

"I knew you were looking at my ass."

"Was not."

"Were too," Delany said. They both laughed.

Jade tried to concentrate on the movie, but her mind kept going back to the kiss. And wow—Jade's stomach clenched—what a kiss it was.

❖

Isobel presses up against Heather, her bare breasts snug against Heather's back. The silky smoothness of Heather's skin causes Isobel's nipples to harden. She pushes in closer and wraps her arms around the warmth of the woman sleeping next to her. She is happy and content to just listen to her breathe.

Heather stirs and rolls toward her. "Morning," she whispers, and kisses Isobel softly on the lips.

Isobel smiles at her. "Hello."

"We need to talk."

Isobel nods. Icy fear grips her heart. She fears Heather will tell her that she will be leaving soon.

"Irving sent me to Banchory, to be married."

The breath catches in Isobel's throat.

"I was on my way there when I managed to run away."

"But how?"

"I was in the carriage. 'Tis a long way. We were stopped for the night several days ago. Once everyone was asleep I managed to slip away. I followed the trail back on foot. I hid whenever I heard someone coming. I barely slept at all. All I knew was that I had to get away from them and get back to you."

"What about your brother? Surely he will look for you?"

"He will. We shall have to leave here soon. No place will be safe until we are very far away. Will you go with me?"

"But what of your life here? What of your things?"

"Things? They are only things. I neither want them nor need them. All I need is you and to know that you love me. We can find a way. We can make it work—if you want to be with me as well."

That is the one thing Isobel is sure of, her love and desire for Heather. She will do whatever it takes for them to be together. She will leave her home and her brother to have a life with Heather.

She gives Heather a soft kiss. "Of course I will go with you. We can form a plan and be together forever."

"Oh, Isobel. I was so hoping you would feel that way. When do you think we can take our leave?"

Isobel purses her lips as she thinks. They will need food and water, as well as a blanket. Isobel has few belongs to take, and Heather can't risk going back to her house to get anything. "I think tomorrow night might be best. That will give me a chance to get provisions together."

"I can ask Maura to get some of my clothes for me to bring." Heather raises herself up on her elbows.

"That will not be safe."

"It will be fine. I trust her. She will know what to get."

"But how will she get it without your brother knowing?"

"He is gone from sunup until evening. She will know when to go."

Isobel worries still. The fewer people that know about this, the better. "How would you even get word to her?"

"You could take her a letter."

Isobel shakes her head. "I do not think this is a good idea."

"I can tell you how to find her. The letter will tell her when and where to meet us tomorrow. We could be on our way as soon as night falls."

Isobel heaves a heavy sigh. She will do as Heather asks. The sense of impending doom descends on her, enveloping her in a cloud of fear.

Delany woke up when Jade nudged her.

"You might be more comfortable in your bed than sleeping on that chair."

"You might be more comfortable in my bed, too," Delany said, still half-asleep. That kiss, along with her dream about Isobel and Heather, had affected her more than she was willing to let on.

"What?"

"Nothing. Kidding. Guess I fell asleep, huh?" She sat upright and rubbed her eyes.

"Guess you did. You didn't miss much. Boy meets girl, boy loses girl, boy gets girl back. Only thing that would have made it a better movie was if boy was a girl."

Delany had plenty of those movies, but she hadn't added them to the list she'd offered Jade. She didn't want to go to bed frustrated. That kiss had left her wanting. A romantic movie with lesbians would have put her over the top. Of course, it might have also put Jade over the top and they might have wound up in bed together. No. If Delany was going to sleep with Jade, it was going to be because Jade wanted her, not because Jade was horny from watching a movie. She had made the right decision not to mention them.

"Need help getting upstairs?" Jade asked, still leaning over her.

Delany averted her eyes with great difficulty to keep herself from staring at Jade's cleavage, clearly visible from the way the weight of her breasts pulled her shirt down in front. "Nope. I fell asleep, I didn't pass out drunk. I can do it."

Jade backed up to give her room but offered her hand. Delany reached for it and the warmth sent a tingle through her. She was sure Jade felt it, too. She was going to have a lot of trouble staying in her own bed tonight.

"I need something to write with," Heather says to Isobel.

Isobel looks around the room. The fire from the night before has faded to a smolder. She pulls out a twig that is burnt on one end. "Here." She hands it to Heather.

"What can I write on?" Heather asks.

"Oh wait. I know." Isobel pulls a wooden box from under the bed. The thick layer of dust on top swirls into the air as she opens it. Inside are several pieces of parchment made from the skin of a goat. Isobel chooses one with a faded childish drawing of a cow on it and hands it to Heather.

"What is this?" Heather asks.

"I drew it when I was young. My father would give me scraps of parchment that he sometimes traded vegetables for in the village."

"'Tis quite good, even for a child. Do you still draw?"

Isobel shakes her head. "No. Not since my parents were killed. My uncle thought it foolish."

"I cannot write on your beautiful drawing," Heather says, trying to hand it back to Isobel.

"You must. There is nothing else to use."

Heather takes the drawing and twig to the table. Slowly and deliberately, she writes. When she's done, she rolls it and hands it to Isobel.

"Find Maura. She will be down by the riverbank at this time of day." She tells her the exact location to look. "Isobel, what about Tomas? Will he wonder where you are? Why you were not in your bed when he rose?"

"No. There is many a morning I rise before him and take my leave. He knows I like to spend time away from others. He'll not worry until later—if he does not see me by suppertime."

"After you see Maura, go see Tomas. Make up a story as to where you will be so he'll not worry later. I shall be waiting here for your return."

"Are you truly sure you want me to find Maura? We can make do with what I can gather." Please. Let us not involve Maura, Isobel silently pleads.

Heather takes Isobel's hands in her own. "I tell you, it will be fine. The letter says for her to go to my house, collect what I have listed, then meet us on the ridge before nightfall."

Isobel is lost in the depth of Heather's eyes. She will do whatever she asks of her.

With the parchment in her hand, Isobel kisses Heather on the cheek. Heather's skin is soft beneath her lips, and she lets them linger.

"Take care and come back soon." Heather pulls her into a hug.

"Latch the door behind me and open it for no one."

Heather nods.

"I will return as soon as I am able." She hurries out of the cabin before she has a chance to change her mind. She finds Maura right where Heather said she would be.

"May I talk to you alone?" she asks, trying her best to keep her voice from quivering.

"I think not." Maura turns away from her.

Isobel reaches out to touch her sleeve then thinks better of it. *"Please,"* she says. *"Heather has sent me."*

"Heather?" she whispers, her head still turned away. *"Where is she?"*

Isobel looks at the people around them. *"Please,"* she says again. *"Can we talk alone?"*

Maura turns, squinting at her, a scowl covering her face. *"Meet me behind Sweeny's barn on the hill. Go now, and I shall be along soon."*

Isobel didn't have to wait long for Maura to appear.

"Tell me where she is," Maura demands.

Isobel thrusts the note at her. *"She sent this for you."*

Maura eyes Isobel before unfurling the parchment. *"How do I know this is not a trick and that you yourself did not write this note to fool me?"*

Isobel shakes her head, once again convinced this is a bad idea. *"I do not know how to write. You knew this already. Why on God's green earth would I want to fool you?"*

"Who knows what the likes of you are capable of? Tell me where Heather is."

Isobel thinks for a moment that Maura might strike her if she refuses, but she is willing to take that chance. *"I ask that you bring what Heather has listed. You can see her then."*

"All right. I shall do as this note asks. But I am telling you, as surely as I am standing here, that she had better be there when I arrive."

"She will be." Isobel turns to leave.

"Wait," Maura says. *"Wait until I am well on my way before you go. I do not want to take the chance of anyone seeing me with you."*

Isobel lets out the breath she's been holding as she watches Maura walk away.

She quickly makes her way to her uncle's house and finds Tomas in the garden.

"Nice of you to arrive in time to help me," he says to her. *"You took your leave very early this morn."*

"I am not here to help. I wanted to let you know I would not be home for supper tonight. A new friend has invited me to eat with her family." Isobel cringes inside at the lie.

Tomas looks up from his work. *"What new friend?"*

"Her name is Lara. We met at the marketplace days ago. She is most welcoming and invited me for today."

"And you only think to tell me this the day you are to go?"

"Sorry. I forgot."

Tomas shakes his head and smiles. *"All right then, off with you, lass. Be home by nightfall."*

"I will," Isobel says. She is shaking by the time she reaches the trail through the woods that will take her back to Heather.

She quietly unlatches the door and enters, closing it behind her. There is no one there. She realizes Heather is not in the cabin. For a moment Isobel fears she will vomit from worry. Did Irving find her and take her away? Did she leave the cabin and get hurt, unable to return? A cold panic grips her heart, making it hard to breathe.

Isobel rushes outside. She doesn't know if she dares call out her name. Running through the woods, she looks continually side to side, behind trees and rocks, in a desperate attempt to find her. Finally, she can't take it anymore and calls out Heather's name.

"Shh," a voice says behind her. It's Heather.

Isobel sobs at the sight of her.

Heather puts down the old wooden bucket she is carrying

and pulls Isobel into her arms. She whispers over and over, "What is it, Isobel?"

"I thought..." Isobel sobs. "I thought you...were gone. I thought I had lost you."

"Oh, Isobel. I am sorry. I took leave of the cabin to pick berries. Hunger got the better of me." She kisses her forehead and wipes the tears from her cheeks. "Oh, my sweeting, I am so sorry."

Isobel finds she can't stop the tears. She sucks in gulps of air in an attempt to control the sobs. Feeling light-headed, she might well fall over if not for Heather's arms around her.

It seems to take forever for her to get her crying and breathing back under her control. "I was so scared," she says at last.

"Isobel, you will never lose me."

Delany rolled over in her bed, replaying the vision in her mind. They were always so clear, and this one was no exception. She had tears on her cheeks from Isobel's sobs. Her body reacted to her soul's pain from so long ago. She thought of Jade so close, yet so far away.

Chapter Twenty-Two

Jade lay in bed staring up into the darkness. Delany was right down the hall. How easy it would be to slip into her room and into her bed. Jade found herself wet at the very thought of it.

She pictured herself kissing Delany, tongues intertwined, dancing a desperate waltz of need. Closing her eyes, she undressed Delany in her mind and stepped into her, feeling her nakedness press against her. She imagined her hands on Delany, her fingers moving through her hair, down her back, across her breasts. Her hand wandered down her own body in reality as it traveled down Delany's in her fantasy. She could feel how wet she was and considered pleasuring herself for relief. But she knew that wasn't what she wanted, and it wouldn't make this ache go away. Only being with Delany would help, and that wasn't going to happen—at least not tonight. She had a lot of things to think about, a lot of things to figure out before she could let that happen—if she could let it happen at all.

She rolled over on her side and pulled the extra pillow to her chest. To her surprise, tears sprang to her eyes. She let them fall in the darkness, not knowing exactly what she was crying for.

❖

A light knock on the door woke Jade from a sound sleep. She opened her eyes, surprised by the sunlight streaming through the sheer curtains. Clearing her throat, she said, "Come in." She sat up.

Delany opened the door wide enough to pop her head in. "Sorry to wake you. I started breakfast a while ago. I didn't want it to get cold, so I thought maybe I should get you up. Hope that's okay."

"That's more than okay. I'd gladly be awakened by a beautiful woman making me breakfast." She resisted the urge to put her arms out to Delany and invite her into them.

"Thanks for the compliment. Get your lazy ass out of bed and come join me. Leave your pajamas on. You can shower and get dressed later," Delany said with a smirk.

Jade's pajama top was one of Delany's old T-shirts. The slightest breeze—or thought of Delany—would send her nipples to full attention and poking through the material. "Do you happen to have a bathrobe I can wear?"

"In the closet." Delany pointed. "Meet you downstairs."

Delany gently pulled the door closed and headed down the stairs. *No need for a bathrobe now*, she thought. *I've already gotten an eyeful.* It was all she could do to keep her attention on Jade's face as she talked to her. That tight shirt hid nothing. It was also all Delany could do to keep from crossing the room and crawling into bed with her. That kiss last night had reawakened all the thoughts and desires that Delany had been trying desperately to push down and control. She wasn't sure what she was going to do with all those feelings. She wasn't about to lose Jade by letting her know how much she wanted her—body and soul.

Their souls had been intertwined before as Heather and Isobel. There wasn't a doubt in Delany's mind. They had loved each other in that lifetime, and they could love each other in this one. At least, that's what Delany wanted.

She could feel the joy and the fear Isobel felt loving Heather. But she could also feel the joy and the fear she herself felt around Jade. They were separate and distinct in her mind and her heart.

She was afraid her feelings would go unanswered, that Jade wouldn't feel the same for her. But then there was that kiss last night. What was that all about? Jade had kissed her. Kissed her fully and thoroughly. There was no mistaking that. So many thoughts and emotions ran through her head. What about what the psychic said? That Jade did have feelings for her but was afraid. How could Delany help put her fears to rest?

The frustration grew with each question. Delany looked up toward the ceiling and let out a sound that was half grunt and half groan.

"Wow," Jade said, coming into the room. "That bad, huh?"

Delany shook her head and laughed at being caught. "Just life."

"I hear ya. Hard to figure out sometimes." Jade pulled out a chair and plopped down. "I'm here for breakfast. Rumor has it, this place serves good food."

"Rumor is correct. We have bacon, eggs, pancakes, French toast, waffles…you name it, we got it."

"Really?"

"No. Not really. What do you think this is? A restaurant? I made pancakes. Bacon will be ready in a minute." She set a cup of coffee down in front of Jade and a container of half-and-half next to it.

"Can I help with anything?"

"Nope. I've got it covered." Jade looked cute in the bathrobe, and Delany smiled at the thought of what it was covering up. She had brushed her hair and put it in a ponytail before coming down.

"What should we do today?"

"Hmm," Delany said out loud, but her thoughts said something different. *How about I take you back upstairs and rip that bathrobe off, for starters? Then we'll remove the rest of the clothes standing between us and I'll have my way with you? Huh?* "Anything special you had in mind?"

"You mentioned the art gallery. That sounds like it might be fun."

Delany took the bacon from the frying pan and laid it out on paper towels to drain. "The Memorial Art Gallery has an exhibit of Georgia O'Keeffe's work right now."

"Isn't she the one who painted the extreme close-ups of flowers that look like lady parts?"

Delany laughed. "Lady parts? You mean vaginas?"

Jade giggled and Delany found it endearing. "Yes, those would be the lady parts. That's what my mom always called it when I was growing up. Sometimes I slip back into that little-girl mode when I least expect it."

"Your little-girl mode is cute. And yes, she's the one, but she has a lot of different work, too. She's done quite a few abstracts that don't get nearly as much attention." Delany set two plates of food on the table and sat down.

"Thanks. This looks great. And seeing lady parts later sounds great, too."

Delany watched the blush creep up Jade's neck to her cheeks.

"I mean the lady part flowers. Flowers. Paintings of flowers—and abstracts."

"Uh-huh," Delany said, with a grin.

Isobel wipes her hand across her mouth to catch a drop of juice from the fresh berries she's sharing with Heather. She leans back on the bench and settles against the table. "I'm sorry I didn't think to bring us back something to eat. I was so worried about meeting Maura and then talking to Tomas. I completely forgot. I hated lying to him."

Heather takes both of Isobel's hands and holds them in her lap. The mere touch makes Isobel feel better—calmer. Like everything is going to be all right.

"I am sorry you had to do that. You can always change your mind about coming away with me. I do not want you to be hurt in any way, and I know leaving Tomas hurts you."

Isobel shakes her head. Leaving Tomas will not be easy, but losing Heather would be unbearable. "I want to be with you. I know we must leave here to do that."

"Oh, Isobel. My heart threatens to burst from my chest with the love I have for you." She leans over and kisses Isobel on the cheek. Isobel turns her head, capturing Heather's lips. She trembles as the soft kiss grows deeper. Passion ignites in her belly, urging her onward. She stands, pulling Heather up with her, never breaking the kiss. Her hands tug at clothing, both hers and Heather's, in a hurried attempt to remove it.

When the last piece of clothing falls to the floor, Isobel steps back and looks at the woman standing before her. The woman she loves with all her heart. The woman she wants to love with her body as well. The beauty of her infiltrates every cell of Isobel's being, and she is engulfed in the heat of her.

It takes all of her willpower to stand where she is. She reaches out and lets her fingertips caress Heather's face, her neck, her collarbone. Slowly, her hand glides downward, memorizing every curve, every crease, every sensation.

Heather tilts her head back and moans as the fingers sweep across her nipples. Isobel pauses and whispers, "Look at me. I want to see your eyes. I want to look into your very soul."

Heather obeys, and Isobel's fingers continue on their journey until they are in the tight curl of blond hair between Heather's thighs.

"Look at me," Isobel repeats softly, even though Heather's eyes have not left hers.

A deep moan leaves Heather's throat as Isobel's fingers glide through the slick folds and enter her. Slowly at first, allowing Heather's wetness to coat her fingers, then with more speed, going deeper with every thrust.

Isobel steps closer, wrapping her other arm around Heather's neck and bringing her head down until their mouths are united in a deep kiss.

Delany shook the image from her head but had trouble shaking the feeling from her body. She splashed cold water on her face. Jade was downstairs waiting for her so they could go to the museum. She looked at herself in the mirror and smiled. Heather and Isobel were together in her vision and she would be spending the day with Jade. Life was good.

❖

"Looks like a lady part to me," Jade said, staring at the painting. Maybe art just wasn't her thing. She didn't see the point to most of what she was seeing.

Delany laughed. "Yep. It does." She glanced at the guidebook. "I'm surprised they don't have more of her flower paintings. This is the only one."

"What do you think of it?" Jade asked.

"Well, I certainly like lady parts, so I have to say, I like the painting. I think some of her abstracts look like vaginas too. Like this one." Delany pointed to another painting. "It's called *Grey Line with Black, Blue, and Yellow.* It should have been called *Colorful Vagina.*"

"Or *Rainbow Lady Parts*," Jade added with a chuckle.

"Or *Lively Labia.*" Delany snickered.

"Or *Vivid…*" Jade had trouble speaking, trying to suppress a laugh. "*Vulva.*"

"Can I answer any questions for you ladies?" the gallery docent asked, coming up behind them.

Delany wiped a tear from her cheek and cleared her throat. "Um, no. We were admiring this painting."

Jade giggled and Delany elbowed her.

"Ah, yes. A beautiful piece. It's part of the traveling exhibit on loan from the Museum of Fine Arts in Houston. It's one of Miss O'Keeffe's finest pieces. If you look closely you can see the delicate strokes made by her own hand."

Jade put her hand over her mouth to try to control the laughter that was bubbling up, but to no avail. It came tumbling out.

"I'm so sorry," Delany told the guide. "My friend here has no appreciation for art. I brought her here in an attempt to expand her horizons, but apparently, it did no good. All she sees is lady parts when she looks at these paintings." Delany didn't crack a smile.

A small sound, a cross between a cough and a cackle, left Jade's throat before she could swallow it back down in her attempt not to laugh. The guide looked from her to Delany and back again. Jade was sure he had no idea if Delany was being serious or not.

"Yes. I see," he said, after a long pause. "Alrighty then. Let me know if you have any questions." He strode away in the direction he had come from.

"I have more questions," Jade said to Delany, when he was out of earshot. "Should I go get him?"

Both women burst out laughing. "I don't think so," Delany said, when the laughing subsided. "I think he's probably given out all the information he can handle today."

"We're lucky we didn't get kicked out."

"Something tells me you'd have been okay with that. Not getting much out of this, are you?"

Jade took Delany by the elbow. "To be honest, the paintings don't do much for me. But I'm still having a wonderful time." She was happy just being with Delany. "Do you like this?"

"I do. I used to draw when I was a kid. I like seeing what other people have done with art. But we don't have to stay."

"No. I want to see the rest. Explain it to me. I'm willing to learn." She looked into Delany's eyes—beautiful eyes—and smiled. "Please."

"Okay. I'm no expert, but this piece"—she strolled over to

the next painting—"is called *My Backyard*. Tell me what you see?"

Jade looked closely at the painting. The brown and blue tones definitely looked like mountains and sky. And the green in the front resembled trees or maybe bushes. "It looks like a landscape, but there's not a lot of detail in it."

"It is. It's New Mexico. It's almost abstract in its lack of detail."

"Is it bad to say it looks like it was done by a fourth grader?"

Delany smiled. "No. It does kind of look like that. But at the same time, it's almost lyrical. Magical. It's real and yet it's not quite. Make sense?"

Jade was starting to see what Delany was talking about. The painting started taking on a whole new meaning. She nodded.

"It's called *My Backyard* because it was very personal to her. This was what she saw around her where she lived. Look at how subtle the colors are. That's why seeing things like this in person is important. You don't get a true image of what the original looks like by seeing it online or in print."

"I see what you're talking about. When I really look at it, I can see all the colors she used and how she blended them. Remarkable." Jade smiled at Delany, thankful for her taking the time to explain what she hadn't been exposed to before. It gave her a whole new appreciation for art—and for Delany. Maybe it was time to explore what was right in front of her.

CHAPTER TWENTY-THREE

"If I buy you an O'Keeffe print, will you actually hang it up in your house?" Delany asked later as they meandered through the gift shop.

"You don't have to do that," Jade answered.

"I know I don't *have* to. I want to. Would you? Be honest with me."

Be honest with her. I haven't been honest about my feelings, that's for sure. Jade wondered if she should tell her. Maybe it would be a good idea to think about things once she got home and had some alone time. If she still felt the same way about Delany once there was some space between them, then she could decide what to do.

"Earth to Jade," Delany said. "I won't get it if you don't like it."

"Yes, I would hang it in my house. Which one were you thinking?"

"That depends. Want one with lady parts or one without lady parts?"

Jade smiled. "You decide."

"Hmm. I'm choosy about whose lady parts I see, and I'm not sure I would want to be looking at Georgia O'Keeffe's. So, let's get one without."

Delany picked out a print, double-checked with Jade for her approval, and paid for it. "All ready?" Delany asked her.

"In a few. Why don't you go wait in the lobby and I'll be right out."

Delany raised her eyebrows. "What are you up to?"

"Never you mind. I'll only be a few minutes." She pushed Delany in the direction of the door. As soon as she was out of sight, Jade went back to the art kits she had seen earlier and picked out one that contained drawing pencils, sketch paper, and an instruction book.

With her purchase bagged and tucked under her arm, she joined Delany in the lobby. "All set," she told her.

If Delany noticed the bag, she didn't say anything about it.

❖

Delany hated to see the weekend come to an end. "I had such a nice time with you. I hope we can do this again soon."

Jade gathered her few belongings and the O'Keeffe print. "Me too. I got this for you." She handed over the bag from the gift shop.

"What is it?"

"Guess you have to open it to find out."

Delany reached into the bag and pulled out the drawing set. "That was so sweet of you," she said, truly touched, ignoring the impulse to pull Jade into a tight hug.

"I expect you to use it. I want to see a masterpiece the next time I visit."

Next time. Delany's heart swelled at the thought.

"I'll give it a shot, but I think a masterpiece isn't in my near future." She looked up at Jade. "But I'm hoping you will be. Would I be pushing it if I suggested I take a trip to see you next weekend?" She waited, anticipating Jade to turn her down. If she was expecting a negative answer, then she wouldn't be disappointed when it happened. Right?

"That would be great."

"Really?" Delany tried to keep the excitement from her voice.

"Yes, really. Don't act so surprised."

But Delany *was* surprised. First she'd been surprised Jade had shown up for the weekend, and now she was surprised she was agreeing to get together again so soon. *Watch your heart*, her head told her again. But she didn't listen. She was going to get to spend more time with Jade. That was all she cared about.

"Draw me something right now," Jade said.

Delany shook her head. "Uh, no. I haven't drawn since I was a kid."

"Draw something you drew when you were a kid. I want something to take home with me."

"I bought you that print to take."

"I mean your art. I want to take *your* art. It doesn't have to be complicated. Whatever you want to draw is fine."

Delany sat at the kitchen table, flipped the sketch pad open, and drew one of the things she loved to draw when she was a kid. She signed her name at the bottom, tore the sheet off, and handed it to Jade.

"It's a picture of a cow," Jade said. "I love it."

Isobel gathers what she needs and packs it into the leather satchel. Tomas won't be back from the fields for some time, and her uncle will be out even later than that. She takes enough food for several days and a bladder of water they can refill when it's empty.

They don't know for sure where they're going but know that south would probably be best. They have their story worked out. They're sisters trying to get to relatives after the death of their parents. Once they're far enough away, they'll get jobs as house servants or in the fields. They'll do whatever it takes to survive as long as they are together. Isobel hoists the bag across her shoulders and looks around at what has been her home since she was a child. She will not miss this place, for it never felt truly hers. It was Uncle's, and she had been begrudgingly allowed to live here. She will, however, miss Tomas with all her heart. Tears spring to her eyes and she wipes them away with disdain. There is no time for that now. She must focus on the task at hand. Her thoughts turn to Heather, and she heads to the cabin.

Heather's inside when she returns. She unpacks a bit of the food she has brought and sets it out for them to eat.

"Did anyone see you?" Heather asks, between bites.

"No. I shall have to go back before nightfall so Tomas does not come looking for me. I shall sneak out again as soon as he is asleep."

"I know how hard it is for you to leave him, Isobel. I am so very sorry."

Isobel fights back the tears. Yes, it will be hard. A part of her heart is breaking at the thought, but she knows she must do it in order to be with Heather. "You're leaving your brother, too," she reminds her.

"He and I are not close like you and Tomas."

"I will miss him. That is true. Maybe someday we can see each other again. For now, this is how it must be." She takes Heather's hand in hers. "You are my one true love, and where you go, I go."

"It is the same for me, my love." Heather raises Isobel's hand to her lips and kisses it. "So, we will be set to leave tomorrow night. Maura will meet us on the ridge with the things I requested."

Fear grips Isobel's heart at the mention of Maura. She prays Heather's trust in her is not misplaced.

❖

Jade turned the radio in her car louder to drown out the noise from the traffic around her. She hummed along to the music, using her steering wheel as a drum to hammer out the beat.

She knew she had things to figure out, preferably before next weekend when Delany came to visit. She smiled at the thought. She realized she had been smiling a lot that weekend. There was still an edge of fear to the whole thing that she couldn't quite understand. She chose to ignore it.

She was still thinking about it when she put her key in the front door and was greeted by Cliché. "Hey, buddy boy. Did you miss me?"

He rubbed up against her legs, threatening to trip her. She bent down and scooped him up, but he immediately jumped out of her arms.

"Well, then," she said. "Make up your mind. Do you love me or not? You are so fickle. Maybe that's what Delany thinks about me. I'll bet she's having a heck of a time figuring me out." Jade picked up Cliché's water dish, dumped the water, and refilled it. "I know I'm having a heck of a time trying to figure myself out."

Cliché was back rubbing against her legs. "Looking for some fresh food?" Jade poured more dry food over what was already in the bowl. The cat devoured it as if he hadn't eaten in a week.

"Okay, Cliché, help me figure this out." Cliché didn't look up from the bowl. "I like her. I mean, really like her. That much I know. I know she likes me. What's stopping me from pursuing this?"

Cliché didn't answer.

"Exactly. Nothing. That's why I like talking to you. You have all the answers. So next weekend, when she's here, I should tell her. Right? That's okay," she said to the cat. "You don't have to answer. I've got this one. The answer is yes. I'll make us a nice dinner, candles, soft music—the whole thing—and somewhere around dessert, I'll tell her."

❖

They reach the top of the ridge at midmorning with time to spare before Maura is to arrive. Isobel carries the meal she has prepared for them. Heather spreads a small green plaid blanket on the ground and motions for Isobel to sit. They enjoy their meal together as they wait.

"I am in need of a chamber pot," Heather says, with a laugh. "But since there are none to be found out here, I will have to find a tree to go behind." She stands to take her leave. "I shan't be long." She heads off down the hill.

Isobel begins to gather the scraps from her meal when she hears someone coming up the hill from the opposite side that Heather went down. She stands, believing it must be Maura. Her breath catches in her throat as the person comes into view.

Irving.

Her thought is to run, but her legs won't move.

"Where is she?" Irving bellows. "Where is my sister?"

"I...I...do not..."

"Do not lie to me, you little arse. Tell me where she is before I kill you. Maura said she would be here. Now, where is she?" He pulls a slingshot, forged from a tree branch, from his back pocket. He picks up a rock half the size of his hand from the ground.

Isobel turns to run as he loads it into the slingshot and pulls it back.

Searing pain shoots through Isobel's leg as the rock slams into the back of her calf. Her ripped skin leaks blood onto the warm ground. She looks up into the eyes of a madman as he drops the slingshot and charges at her. She ducks and slips under his huge, outstretched arms, his fingers skimming across her neck, leaving a trail of scratches. The world blurs as she turns and blindly pushes at him with the full weight of her body. He teeters, already off balance from missing his target. His arms flail helplessly, trying to stop his forward momentum. Loose rocks dislodge as his feet slip out from under him and he tumbles over the edge of the cliff. She stares in disbelief as his massive body disappears from sight. Isobel thinks the bloodcurdling scream she hears is coming from her own throat until she turns toward the sound and sees Heather—eyes bulging, mouth wide open.

"Heather." Isobel runs to her.

"We have to help him," Heather screams.

"Heather," she repeats. She takes Heather by the arms and looks directly into her eyes. "If he is gone, he cannot hurt us anymore. We can be free."

Heather trembles. "No," she screams. "We must get help."

Isobel can't understand why they can't just leave him to die if he's not already dead. This could be the answer to their problems. With Irving dead and out of the way, they can stay here. They can live here, in the cabin. Safe. She wouldn't have to leave Tomas. Doesn't she see that? They can stay.

"Help him!" Heather screams again.

Maura appears as if out of nowhere. She must have come with Irving, Isobel realizes.

"She killed him," Maura yells, pointing at Isobel. "Killed him."

"What? I did not." She looks at Heather, but Heather stares past her to the edge of the cliff. "I did not. He came at me—"

"Liar," Maura shrieks.

"Help him."

Isobel is torn. She doesn't know what to do to help him, and she fears he's already dead. More than that, she fears he may not be. She releases Heather's arms and limps to the edge of the cliff, trying to look over the ridge. She can't see down to the bottom from here. It would be a long way around to get down there.

She wants him to be gone.

She wants him to be dead.

Why can't Heather want that, too? He was evil.

She turns back. "Heather, I do not know what we can do. I cannot see him."

Isobel returns to Heather's side and puts her arm around her shoulder. Heather shakes it off. "You killed him. You killed my brother."

"He was rushing at me. He was trying to kill me."

"Liar. The devil's words come from her very lips," Maura says. "She wanted him gone. She has said as much herself. I bear witness to the whole thing. I saw her kill him. All he wanted was to find you. To assure your safety."

Isobel ignores Maura's words, but Heather does not.

"You swear this to be true?"

"On my very life," Maura lies.

"Heather," Isobel pleads. "Listen to me—"

"No!" Heather's eyes widen. "We have to get help," she screams again and starts down the hill, Maura at her side, Isobel right behind them.

Delany woke with a start. Her breath came heavy from deep in her chest. She sat upright in the dark. She had killed Irving. Isobel had killed him. But she was Isobel. She could still feel his rough shirt as she pushed against him, see his eyes as he lost his balance and tumbled over the cliff. It was as real as if it had just happened.

He had to have died from the fall. There was no way anyone could survive that. Was there any way for her to find out? Doubtful, seeing as it happened five and a half centuries ago. She had killed somebody in a past life. Not just *somebody,* but the brother of the woman she loved.

She reached down and rubbed the spot on the back of her leg where the rock had hit her—hit Isobel. It was painful to the touch. She shook her head. How could being hit with a rock hundreds of years ago when she inhabited a different body cause pain in her leg now? She turned on the light and pulled up the leg of her pajama bottoms. There was no bruise or welt, but the pain was real. She realized it was in the same area that had bothered her when she went to Abby for a Reiki treatment.

If their past life had anything to do with this one, Delany wasn't surprised Jade didn't want a relationship with her. Who would want to be with a murderer? Okay, Delany wasn't actually a murderer. For that matter, neither was Isobel. She was trying to protect herself.

Delany understood that. She wasn't sure Heather had.

She wasn't sure Jade would either. That is, if she ever told Jade any of this.

How could she tell her? Jade would probably think she was nuts. Delany wasn't willing to take that chance. Jade had taken a step toward her, even if it was only in friendship—well, friendship with a hell of a kiss thrown in. Delany didn't want to do anything to mess that up.

Maybe it would be best if she could somehow get over her own feelings for Jade and really just be her friend. She wasn't sure how to go about doing that. Someone had told her, years ago, that the best way to get over someone was to get under someone else. Maybe that was what she should do. Not necessarily go out and sleep with someone, but maybe start dating. Get her mind off Jade. God knows, Jade was never far from her thoughts. It might not be a good idea to go to Buffalo next weekend. Let more time pass between visits. That might give Delany's heart a chance to calm down.

❖

Jade stopped to visit Uncle Willy after work and had only been home a few minutes when her phone rang. She was happy to see it was Delany calling, but her happiness soon faded when Delany told her she wouldn't be coming for that visit they had planned.

Jade's heart sank. "No, that's okay. If you can't make it, we can plan another time," she said into the phone.

"I'm sorry. I just have too much to do."

Jade had already planned out the dinner menu and exactly how to go about telling Delany her feelings. It would just have to wait, she supposed. It wasn't the kind of thing she wanted to tell her over the phone.

"How about the weekend after that? I have a tennis game planned, but I could easily change it."

"You go ahead and play. We can get together another time."

Jade wasn't sure what to say. She wanted to see Delany and tell her how she felt. Now she was looking at weeks before she would be able to do that. "I can reschedule. Honest."

"Hey listen, I've got to get going. We'll talk again soon. Okay?"

"Sure." Jade tried to keep her voice light.

"Great. Gotta go. Bye."

"Bye." Jade hit the End button and stared at the phone in her hand. "What just happened?"

A few days ago Delany seemed eager to spend time with her. Now she not only canceled their plans but acted like she couldn't get off the phone fast enough.

Jade looked through her contact list and pressed one of the numbers. It was answered on the third ring.

"Hey, Jade. What's up?"

"Hi, Abby. Is there anything going on with Delany?"

"Not that I know of. Why?"

"I don't know. She canceled plans we had and acted like she didn't want to talk to me."

"You didn't do anything to upset her, did you?"

The irritation rose from Jade's stomach to her throat. She worked to keep her voice even. "No. We had a great weekend—at least, I thought we did. We made plans for next weekend. Out of the blue, she calls and cancels them. That doesn't seem like her."

"Not sure what to tell you. Maybe something came up. She didn't talk to me about it."

Jade shook her head. "Something didn't seem right."

"Want me to ask her?"

"Please don't. Don't tell her I called you. I'm probably being stupid."

"Let's flip the question around. What's going on with you? It isn't like you to get upset when someone changes plans."

Jade didn't want to tell Abby about her feelings, at least not until she had a chance to tell Delany. "Nothing."

"You never were a very good liar. You also never were one to share your feelings, so I'll drop it. I'm here if you decide you want to talk about it."

It was true. There was always a part of Jade that didn't trust other people, even as good a friend as Abby, with her innermost thoughts and feelings. But she was willing to lay that on the line with Delany. She had decided to tell her and trust her. Now she wasn't sure when she would get the chance.

"Thanks, Abby. Just trying to figure some things out. No big deal."

"Uh-huh." Abby always could see right through her. "I haven't talked to Delany since we all went out to dinner. She seemed fine then."

"That's the thing. I thought everything was fine, but she seemed kind of weird on the phone a few minutes ago."

"Maybe I should call her."

"Ahh…"

"I won't tell her I talked to you about any of this."

Isobel pulls the collar of her cloak up higher around her neck to keep the chill out as the cold rain pelts against her face, soaking her hair and plastering it to her scalp. She stands back from the crowd of mourners, her attention only on Heather.

Isobel hasn't talked to her since several of the local men pulled Irving's body from the ravine. She went to her house, but Heather refused to come to the door.

The last rock is placed on the grave and the crowd begins to scatter. Isobel approaches Heather as she stands and talks with a couple from the town. Isobel waits, her heart pounding so hard, it threatens to break through her chest. When, at last, the man and woman go, Isobel is afraid Heather may leave without talking to her. But she doesn't.

"How are you?" Isobel asks.

"My brother is dead. That is how I am."

Isobel swallows back the bile that has risen to her throat. "I miss you. Please know how much I love you. I never meant for this to happen."

Heather's eyes soften for the briefest moment. "Do you not see? Our love did this. My brother is dead because I loved you."

Isobel winces at the past tense. "Please say you love me still. I know you do." It's more of a plea than a question.

"We cannot be together."

"Please, Heather. Do not say such a thing."

"Our love must be evil to have caused such as this."

"Our love did not cause this." Isobel trembles. Her heart is breaking. She fears it could stop beating at any moment. "Your brother's hatred caused this."

"I shall not have you speak ill of the dead. I will be leaving in the morning."

Isobel chokes back a sob. No, this can't be. She can't lose Heather. She can't.

"I have decided to do as Irving wished. I am to be married."

Isobel reaches for Heather's hand. She knows if she can get her to listen she can convince her to stay, convince her that their love is all that matters.

Heather pulls away. "No. I'm leaving. There is nothing more to say."

"Please Heather. I love you." The tears are flowing freely now, mixing with the rain and falling to the ground.

Without another word, Heather turns and walks away.

Isobel watches her go, her head spinning, her heart shattered, and she falls to the ground and sobs.

Delany took a couple of personal days off from work. She felt like there had been a death in the family. The loss for Isobel was a loss for her as well. Isobel's pain was her own. She didn't know if this was the end of the story with Heather. The memories came when they came. She had no way of forcing them or speeding them up.

She hadn't talked to Jade in several days. She couldn't. Jade had called a couple of times, and Delany let it go to voicemail. She didn't trust herself not to let the whole story come spilling out of her mouth. She didn't think Jade would understand. She wasn't sure *she* understood. How could something that happened so long ago, literally in another lifetime, affect her so much? Was that all there was to it? She didn't know.

She was trying to get Jade out of her system. Maybe Isobel losing Heather only added to the hurt that Delany already felt. "Ugh," she said out loud, as she sat at the edge of the lake. Being by the water usually helped clear her head. She'd been there half the day, but clarity still evaded her. She couldn't be sure that Heather and Isobel never found each other again. But did that even matter now? What mattered now was her and Jade—the same two souls but with very different lives than Heather and Isobel faced.

Could she remain friends with Jade, when she had such strong feelings for her? Sometimes she was sure she could, that the most important thing was to keep Jade in her life in any way possible. Other times, she thought it was a losing battle. There were times when they were together that it was all Delany could do to keep from touching her, from kissing her.

She shook her head. This was getting her nowhere. She needed to come to some kind of conclusion here and do her best to stick to it.

She stared into the water and listed her options off in her head. She could tell Jade she had feelings for her on the off chance that Jade was open to that. No.

She could go on as they were, as friends. Could she, though? That was the real question. If she could, fine, that would be a good plan. But she found the more time she spent with Jade, the more she wanted to spend with her. That was anything but friendship. That was the beginning of a love affair. And if Delany was the only one with feelings, it was the beginning of heartache, too.

So that left only one option: Stop seeing Jade altogether. It would hurt, but it wouldn't hurt as much as it would a month from now or a year from now. She couldn't grieve the loss of Jade if Jade was still in her life. That was what she needed to do: Grieve the loss, even if it was only the loss of a fantasy.

Delany's eyes welled up with tears. The lake seemed to waver and swim before her. She didn't want to be sobbing in public, but she seemed to have no choice. Despite her objections, the tears ran like rivers down her cheeks.

Why did life have to be so hard? Why couldn't she have what she wanted—the woman she wanted? She cried for Jade, for Heather and Isobel, for the losses she felt in both worlds.

❖

Jade closed the folder and put it into the filing cabinet. She made a quick stop at her secretary's desk to tell her she was leaving before heading off to lunch. She walked the two blocks to her favorite café and found a seat in the last booth, glad for the solitude it afforded her.

She hadn't heard from Delany in several days. Her phone calls went unanswered and she had stopped leaving voicemails after the second one. Delany was obviously avoiding her. She just didn't know why or what to do about it.

She considered skipping lunch and ordering ice cream instead. Drowning her sorrows in sugar seemed reasonable, but maybe not sensible, her thighs informed her. Her thighs won out and she ordered a salad. The extra creamy blue cheese dressing she ordered on the side was to show her thighs who was boss.

Maybe she should drive down to Rochester and tell Delany how she felt. Or not. Jade would be in for a whole lot of embarrassment if she proclaimed her feelings only to have

Delany shut her down. What if she never got another chance to tell her? She would regret that for the rest of her life. She had to take the chance. Now all she had to figure out was how. It had to special. Delany was special, and she deserved something worthy of that.

Maybe she should tell Abby about this after all. She was going to need her help if this was going to work. With Delany's apparent change of attitude, Jade knew she would be taking a risk. But she was going to take a leap of faith and hope she didn't land flat on her face.

CHAPTER TWENTY-FOUR

E verything was in place and ready to go. At least Jade hoped it was. She looked at the time. It was a few minutes before noon. Abby and Delany would be arriving any minute. It was almost show time. She tucked herself away in the back room and waited.

❖

Delany pushed her plate of barely touched food off to the side. Her appetite wasn't what it should be.

"Want me to box that up for you?" the waitress said. She put their bill face down on the table.

"That would be great."

"Any dessert for the two of you? We have a carrot cake that is to die for."

"None for me," Delany answered.

Abby smiled. "That sounds wonderful. One piece and two forks. Please."

"You got it." The waitress left, taking Delany's plate of food with her.

"You didn't eat much," Abby said.

Delany shrugged.

"I paid for lunch the last time. So, it's your turn." Abby slid the check toward Delany.

Delany searched her brain trying to remember whose turn it actually was. She was pretty sure it was Abby's but wasn't going to argue with her. She pulled out her credit card and placed it on top of the bill.

"You're not going to look at it?"

"What's the difference? I'm sure it's right."

"How are you going to know what to leave for a tip?"

What the hell? Was Abby extra annoying today or was everything just getting on Delany's nerves? Delany shook her head. "I was going to leave five dollars. That should be more than enough."

"Maybe not. You should look."

No need to look. Delany was sure five dollars would be a generous amount.

"No, really. You should look."

"What the heck's the big deal?"

"No big deal. Just look."

Better to appease Abby than start an argument, and considering the mood she was in, that might just happen. She turned the bill over. Across it, written in bright red block letters, were the words JADE TAYLOR HAS FEELINGS FOR DELANY PAYTON. Delany flushed with heat as anger seep up from her chest. "That's not very funny, Abby."

Abby opened her mouth to speak but was interrupted by a voice coming from behind Delany.

"It might not be very funny, but it's true."

Delany swung her head around and looked behind her. There stood Jade with a piece of carrot cake in one hand and a bouquet of roses in the other. One single yellow rose sat in the center of a sea of red ones.

Abby stood up. "Time for me to leave. Lots to do today. Thanks for lunch, Delany. One of you better call me later." She kissed Jade on the cheek as she walked past.

Jade slipped into the seat Abby vacated. She handed the flowers to Delany and set the piece of cake on the table.

"Are you going to just stare at me or are you going to say something?"

Delany didn't know what to say. Shock would have been a good word to describe what she felt in that moment.

"Okay. I'll start. But first, you have to close your mouth. I'm afraid a bug might fly in there."

Delany pressed her lips together.

Jade reached over and took Delany's hand. Delany could feel its warmth, and the warmth radiated directly to Delany's heart. She looked into Jade's eyes and waited for her to explain.

"It's true. I do have feelings for you and I would like to explore where those feelings might take us."

Delany's eyes welled with tears. She didn't dare blink for fear they would escape.

"Um. Okay. I was hoping maybe you would say something at this point."

Delany cleared her throat. "I don't understand." She wanted to be sure this was real and she wasn't misinterpreting it.

Jade closed her eyes for a moment and tilted her head back. She took a deep breath and once again looked directly into Delany's eyes.

It felt like Jade was looking into her very soul.

"I know I said I didn't want a relationship, and at the time, it was true. But since I've gotten to spend more time with you, I've come to truly care about you, and I would like to see where this could go."

Delany took a few seconds to let Jade's words sink in.

"Please say something."

Delany blew out the breath she'd been holding. Say something. Should she say what she had been feeling since the first time she met Jade? That she felt like she already knew her and that since that time she found out why?

"Delany?"

"I feel exactly the same way." Now, what about the rest? No, she wouldn't tell her—at least not yet. "I think I have since the moment I first met you." Okay, shouldn't have said that last part.

"I kind of knew that and, well…it scared me a little…and by a little, I mean a lot."

"I'm sorry."

"Please don't be. I was so determined that I didn't want a relationship that I couldn't let it in. It seemed too fast. Does that make sense?"

It made total sense. If someone had told Delany a year ago that she would fall for someone she'd just met, she would have told them they were crazy. But that was exactly what had happened. She wasn't sure she would have believed the rest of it either—the past-life part.

She gave Jade's hand a squeeze. "So, where do we go from here?"

"Well, I would say let's go back to your place." Jade laughed and wiggled her eyebrows up and down. "But I'm not that kind of girl."

"That's not what I hear." Delany had trouble containing her smile.

Jade slapped her arm. "Hey."

"Hey nothing. You wanted me before you ever even met me."

"I'm sorry for all the mixed signals. But now that we've cleared that up, I have a very important question for you."

Delany leaned in closer. "What is it?"

"Are we ever going to eat this piece of carrot cake?"

❖

Jade pulled her phone from her pocket. The text from Abby came right on schedule. She smiled.

Abby: Are you going to tell me what happened?

Jade: How come you're texting me instead of Delany? I thought she filled you in on all this stuff?
Abby: She didn't answer my text. Are the two of you together?
Jade: Nope
Abby: Why not? Where is she? Where are you?
Jade: My parents. Not sure where she is.

Jade laughed. She knew Abby was going nuts not knowing what happened. She was having too much fun stringing her along to stop.

Abby: You're driving me crazy here.
Jade: If you're crazy it wasn't because I drove you there. You've always been a little off.
Abby: JADE!!!
Jade: What?
Abby: Tell me what happened!
Jade: The waitress put the bill on the table and I had written a note on it...
Abby: Damn you! I know that part.
Jade: Oh yeah, you were there.
Abby: So help me, when I get my hands on you...
Jade: OK, OK. It went really well. I was so nervous about what her reaction would be. It took her a few minutes, but she said she wants to give this a try, too.
Abby: Wonderful! So why aren't you together now?
Jade: She had something she had to do. She wasn't very clear. I'm going over to her house in a little while.
Abby: How are you feeling about all this?

Jade thought about it for a moment. Even though she didn't usually share her feelings with anybody, this somehow felt different. She felt different. Like it was okay to let someone else into her heart. She thought she had done that in relationships in the past. Now she wasn't so sure. She wanted it to be different with Delany. She wanted to let her in and to trust her.

Jade: Great. It was the right thing to do.
Abby: Good. I think so, too.

Jade was so glad she had told Delany and so glad Delany felt the same way. This was a new beginning. She couldn't wait to see where it led.

❖

Delany made a couple of quick stops before heading home. Her head was still reeling from Jade's declaration. She wanted to make sure everything was perfect for later. Later. When Jade was there. Jade, who was willing to give this a try.

Delany got everything ready with time to spare. Her phone pinged a text. She looked at it. A third text from Abby. *Probably should respond this time.* She hit Abby's name in her contacts list and Abby answered on the first ring. "So, tell me what's going on."

"Wow. You don't even say hello? You just demand answers?"

"Hello. Now, tell me what's going on."

Delany paced the length of her living room and filled Abby in on the details. "So Jade should be here in about an hour. I'm going to make us dinner."

"And?"

"And what?"

"I don't know. Just and."

"And I don't know. I don't know what to expect. How fast or slow she wants to take this. I've also been trying to figure out how much to tell her about our past life together."

"I think you should tell her all of it. I know you, and if you don't, you're going to feel like it's this big secret between you. It's going to take on a life of its own."

"It already feels like that. I wish I knew how the story ended for Isobel and Heather. The visions stopped. I don't know if they ended up together or if Irving's death drove them apart."

"Does it really matter?"

"It does to me."

"Why don't you concentrate on one thing at a time? If you can't decide on whether to tell Jade or not, play it by ear. If it feels right, tell her. If not, don't."

"You're right. I'm driving myself nuts trying to figure it out." Time for less thinking and more action. She was hoping there would be lots of action soon.

❖

Jade tapped her fingers on the steering wheel and ordered the acid in her stomach out. It wasn't like she and Delany hadn't spent time together before. But this was different. This was for all the marbles. Jade wanted everything to feel perfect. For both of them.

She pulled into Delany's driveway, took a quick look at herself in the rearview mirror, and smoothed down a wayward piece of hair. Taking a deep breath, she opened the door and got out. A few quick adjustments to her clothes and she was ready. For what, she didn't exactly know. She knew Delany was making dinner, but they hadn't discussed it beyond that.

Delany had changed her clothes and looked beautiful in what appeared to be a new pair of tan pants and a sky-blue button-down shirt. Jade accepted the single carnation Delany held out for her.

"Hi," Delany said, almost shyly. "I was going to get you a red rose, but then I figured you might think I'd just pulled one out of the bouquet you gave me."

Jade laughed. "Good thinking." She kissed Delany on the cheek.

Delany pulled her into a hug. She felt so good in her arms.

"How ya doing?" Jade asked. She wasn't sure why she felt the need to make small talk when all she wanted to do was grab Delany by the collar and kiss the living shit out of her.

"Excellent. Now that you're here." She gave her most reassuring smile. "Come in."

Jade followed Delany into the kitchen. It smelled like chicken and roasted potatoes. She leaned against the counter while Delany took her carnation, cut the bottom of the stem, and added it to the vase of roses.

"Beautiful," Jade said.

"Yes, you are." Delany pulled Jade to her by the waistband and into a kiss.

Jade's head swam as Delany's tongue entered her mouth, staking its claim. Jade leaned in against the leg Delany slipped between her thighs. Moisture surged, threatening to soak through her pants onto Delany's. She wanted this woman. She wanted her now.

Finding the edge of Delany's shirt, Jade tugged it upward. Her hand grazed the soft skin on Delany's back.

"Stop." Delany stepped back, away from her and out of her arms.

The heat in Jade's body turned cold in an instant. Unexplainable fear enveloped her. She tried to speak but nothing came out. Tears filled her eyes and threatened to roll down her cheeks.

"Hey." Concern showed on Delany's face and she reached for Jade's arm. "It's okay. I…"

The tears broke over the edge and cascaded down Jade's face. She swiped at them, embarrassed.

"Come here." Delany pulled her back into a hug. "Why are you crying?"

"Damned if I know."

"Oh, sweetie. Everything's all right. I just wanted to talk to you before—well, before we go any further." She pulled back and looked into Jade's eyes. "Nothing's changed. I want to talk. Okay?" She brushed the last of the tears from Jade's cheeks.

Jade nodded. What the hell had come over her? She let Delany lead her by the hand to the living room. They sat side by side on the couch.

Jade waited what seemed like an eternity for Delany to talk, her stomach tight with anticipation.

Delany cleared her throat. Still nothing.

Jade couldn't wait any longer. "Delany. What is it? Just say it."

Delany's smile faltered.

Another stab of fear pierced Jade's heart. Her breath caught in her throat. "If you don't want to do this, please tell me."

This time Delany's smile held firm. "It's not that. I want this. Please know that. But I want to tell you something and I'm afraid you're going to think I'm crazy."

Jade let out a nervous laugh. "I already think you're crazy, so you have nothing to lose. Tell me."

Delany took Jade's hand and ran her fingertips across the back of it. The simple touch not only warmed Jade's heart but made the heat begin to rise once again between her thighs. "For God's sake, Delany."

"When we first met—the first time I saw you—I felt like I knew you. That..." Delany paused.

Jade waited.

"I'm not explaining this well. Let me start over."

"Delany—"

"I know. This is hard. When we met in person you seemed familiar to me, almost like we had met before. But I knew we hadn't. And when we kissed, well, I had sort of this vision..."

"What kind of vision? Like of the future?"

Delany paused. "No. Like from the past."

Jade was confused. "How could you have a vision from the

past if it was the first time we met? Wait. Was it with someone else?"

"Oh, it was you all right. But when I say the past—now here comes the crazy part—I mean a past life. A life we shared together before this one." Delany raised her eyebrows.

Jade was silent, letting Delany's words sink in. She needed more of an explanation because so far this *did* sound crazy. "Go on."

"What I saw when I kissed you was us. Well, not 'us' exactly—I mean it was us. I knew that without a doubt, but we were in different bodies. It was a different time."

Jade listened to the whole story, not saying a word until Delany had completely finished. Her mind told her there was no way any of this could be true. But her heart was screaming out a different opinion. Her heart believed it. She couldn't explain it, but somewhere deep inside her, she knew it was true.

"Say something," Delany pleaded. "Do you think I'm nuts?"

"We've already established that I think that. Now, about your story…"

"It's more than just a story. It's true. I believe that. I would like you to believe it, too. I know it's a lot to swallow. But I had to tell you. I couldn't—"

The rest of the words were swallowed up by Jade's mouth as she kissed her.

❖

Delany allowed herself to be swept up in the kiss as Jade's soft lips took possession of hers. The panic she had felt about telling Jade the truth was being edged out by hot burning desire.

Jade seemed to accept the story without any problems. But how could that be? The story, although true, was unbelievable. But Jade had believed it. Or had she? She hadn't said. She hadn't said much of anything. Delany had no idea what she was thinking.

Suddenly what Jade was thinking became very important. With a great deal of effort and self-control, Delany broke the kiss. She answered the question in Jade's eyes with a question of her own. "I need to know what your thoughts are on all of this."

"It's a lot to take in. Right now, I would rather kiss you than try to figure it out."

"As appealing as that is, I need to know."

"I need some time to let it sink in. There is a part of me that, well…I don't know. That feels like it's true. And if it is, then that would explain the fear I experienced whenever I started to feel close to you."

"Is that why you kept pulling away? Fear?"

Jade nodded. "I didn't understand where it was coming from." It felt good to finally admit it to Delany.

"So, you believe me?"

Jade nodded. Dark brown hair swept across her shoulders. "I know. It's not like me. But I felt something when I met you, too. I didn't realize it at first, but it was there. I was afraid to feel anything for you. If Heather and Isobel lost each other, then maybe that's where my fear comes from. It's kind of mind-blowing."

"I'm not sure if they—we—lost each other. I haven't had any visions since the last one where I—Isobel—this gets confusing—was crying at the graveyard." She paused. "Are you still afraid?"

"Maybe a little." Jade held up her thumb and index finger, holding them slightly apart. She realized she was admitting it to herself as much as she was to Delany.

"You aren't going to lose me. Not this time."

"You aren't going to kill my brother in this lifetime, are you?"

Delany laughed. "You don't have a brother."

"Good point." She placed a gentle kiss on Delany's lips. "There is part of the story I would like to recreate."

Delany couldn't help but grin. "Oh yeah? What part is that?"

"The making love part."

Delany could feel the heat rise from her chest to her face. "I want that, too. But I made dinner and it should be ready any minute. So it's going to have to wait." She attempted to stand up but didn't get more than halfway to her feet when she was yanked back down to the couch by the back of her shirt.

"I'm not hungry...for food," Jade purred in her ear.

The sound from Jade's throat so close to her ear sent a tingle directly to Delany's crotch. The tingle was accompanied by a surge of wetness when Jade's tongue licked the edge of her ear.

Delany let out what she thought was a deep breath but realized was a moan. Her eyes closed as the determined lips licked and sucked their way down her neck. Jade pulled at the material of her shirt and continued down to her collarbone.

Before Delany realized what was happening, Jade had the shirt off her and was pulling at the clasp on the back of her bra. It took only moments for both things to fall to the floor. She sucked in a deep breath as Jade's tongue left a wet line from her shoulder to her breast and she sucked in a nipple.

"Jade," Delany whispered, her voice choking with desire. "Bedroom. Should we...bedroom?"

"Can't...wait...that long." Jade's mouth never left Delany's breast as she pushed her backward until Delany was leaning against the smooth material of the couch. Jade's other hand slid over the seam in Delany's pants, and Delany thought for sure Jade would be able to feel the moisture soaking through them.

Delany unzipped her pants and tried to coax Jade's hand inside.

"Not yet." Jade lifted her head from the nipple she was sucking in and out of her warm mouth. She immediately returned to the task at hand, giving Delany's breast a thorough bathing with her tongue for a few minutes longer.

"Is this what you want?" Jade's hand plunged down the front of Delany's pants, sliding beneath her underwear and into the waiting wetness. "Or should I stop so we can go eat dinner?"

"No. Don't stop," Delany managed to spit out between labored breaths.

"I need these off." Jade slid the pants down past Delany's ankles and tossed them in the pile with her shirt and bra. The underwear followed suit.

Jade lowered her mouth to Delany's pulsating center and snaked her tongue between the folds. Delany parted her legs wider, giving Jade access to her most sacred place.

"Yes," Delany moaned and gripped Jade's head as if she needed to hold her in place. Her breath caught as Jade eased in first one finger, then another, sliding them in and out with the same rhythm as her tongue. Slow at first, then picking up speed and intensity.

Delany's hips lifted from the couch as an orgasm crashed over her. It started in her center, radiating out with more force and power than she had ever experienced before. Her mind went numb for a moment as the waves continued to surge through her.

By the time she was able to open her eyes and focus, she looked down at the beautiful woman still perched between her legs. "Wow," was all she managed to say.

A huge grin spread across Jade's face. "Does that mean you liked it?"

"Um, you could say that. Come here," she said, gently tugging Jade toward her until Jade was leaning on her and they were face-to-face. She kissed her fully on the mouth. "Wow," she said again. "Your turn, as soon as I catch my breath."

"Should I go turn the oven off, so dinner doesn't burn and set the house on fire?"

"Good thinking."

Delany had caught her breath by the time Jade returned. "Let's go upstairs." She took Jade by the hand and led her to the bedroom.

Delany opened her bedroom door and stepped back. Tears sprang to Jade's eyes as she looked in the room. Rose petals on the floor led a path to the bed. More red petals covered the spread and pillows. Ten lit candles were scattered about, giving off the warm scent of vanilla. She turned to Delany. "No one has ever done this for me before. Thank you."

"You deserve it." When she'd set it up earlier, she wasn't sure if Jade would have the chance to see it or not. She was going to let Jade call the shots, and if they hadn't led in this direction she would have just kept the door shut, never letting Jade know the trouble she had gone to.

She took Jade's hand and led her to the side of the bed. She kissed her deeply. Delany unzipped Jade's dress pants and slipped them down to her ankles. She ran her hand up the back of Jade's smooth leg and cupped her ass.

Jade stepped out of her shoes and kicked them, along with her slacks, to the side. She sucked in a rush of breath as Delany's fingers slid over the crotch of her silky underpants.

Delany felt her shiver.

"Oh my God," she moaned.

Delany tugged Jade's shirt up and Jade aided in its quick removal, followed by her bra. Jade's breasts were warm under Delany's hands as her thumbs made deliberate circles around her nipples.

Jade pulled Delany's mouth to her and kissed her deeply. Their tongues danced for control.

Delany's hand vacated one breast, found its way between Jade's legs, and stroked into the wetness.

Jade threw her head back and let out a gasp. She leaned against the bed for support. Jade's legs trembled with each stroke of Delany's hand.

Delany stopped long enough to ease Jade down on the bed and kneel in front of her. "These need to go," Delany said, pulling at the elastic on the sides of Jade's underwear.

Jade stood for Delany to slip them off. The scent of her arousal filled the air. Jade obviously needed no further prompting when Delany pushed her knees apart. She willingly gave Delany full access.

Jade moaned as Delany's tongue swiped across her swollen flesh and then plunged inside her. Jade's sweetness filled Delany's senses. She tasted every part of her center and as far as her tongue could reach.

Jade's breath caught and Delany could tell she was close. Delany increased the pressure and rhythm of her strokes until, finally, Jade exploded against her mouth.

Delany was breathing as hard as Jade was when she came up for air.

Jade pulled her upward.

Delany brought her hand up to her face to wipe away the juices before kissing Jade's mouth.

"Stop," Jade said, taking her hand. She brushed the hair away from Delany's face and lovingly licked the perimeter of her mouth. "All clean," she said, and kissed Delany full on the lips.

No one had ever done that to her before. A new surge of moisture flooded her, her arousal at its highest peak.

"Come here," Jade said, lying back and pulling Delany onto the bed with her. "I've got a thing or two I'd like to do to you."

Chapter Twenty-Five

Delany was just as nervous sitting in the waiting room for the second past-life regression as she'd been the first time around. The biggest difference was that this time Jade was sitting by her side. Her foot tapped out a steady rhythm on the floor.

Jade put her hand on Delany's bouncing knee and smiled. "It'll be fine. Whatever you find out will be fine."

Delany threaded her fingers through Jade's. "Do you believe this? I mean, do you actually believe in past lives?"

"I didn't use to, but I do feel like we've had more than this life together. I can't believe I could feel this much for you if it hadn't started a very long time ago. So I guess the answer is yeah, I believe it."

"What if I find out something bad?" Would it change things in this life? Could it?

"Whatever happened then is over and done with. We have a brand-new chance now. That's what counts."

"You're right. This life is what matters. We are going to do it right." She squeezed Jade's hand.

"You bet your ass we are."

"You kiss your mama with that mouth?" Delany said, with a smile.

"I kiss you with this mouth." Jade leaned over and kissed her on the lips.

"I'm so glad you do."

Their conversation was interrupted as Valerie came out of her office. "I'm ready for you now, Delany," she said.

Jade gave Delany's fingers one final squeeze before releasing them. Delany followed Valerie into the office.

Valerie gave Delany a quick refresher on what they were going to do and Delany reminded her of the lifetime she wanted to visit. Once Delany was stretched out in the chair they began. Valerie went through the relaxation technique and into the past life.

"...so now you are there. Can you see yourself?"

"Yes."

"Heather has told you she's leaving to be married. Where are you?"

"I'm in the graveyard watching her walk away. It's raining."

"What are you feeling?"

"Alone. Scared. I love her. I don't want to lose her. I'm crying." Tears escaped from the corners of Delany's eyes and left a warm trail down her cheeks.

"Is this the last time you ever see Heather?"

"No."

"When do you see her again? What are the circumstances?"

"She's in a carriage."

"What's she doing?"

"She's leaving. She's going to get married and move away. I'm not very close to the carriage. I can see her, but she can't see me. I'm sad and scared."

"Do you ever see her again after that?"

"Yes. Many years later."

"Freeze-frame this moment, and I want you to move ahead to the next time you see Heather again. On the count of three. One...two...three. Immerse yourself in this moment. What's happening now? Where are you?"

Isobel walks down the street with a basket of eggs under her arm. She steps out of the way as a man on a horse rides by. She keeps her head down as she walks avoiding mud puddles from the recent rain.

As she approaches the village, she sees a carriage up ahead, an unusual sight. Only the very rich travel in such a grand manner. It's made of wood with four large spoked wheels and a roof covered in red cloth trimmed with gold fringe. Two horses stand in front at the ready.

Isobel's breath catches in her throat as a woman in her mid-thirties leans forward to look out the window. Their eyes meet. It's Heather.

Heather's eyes brighten with recognition but quickly lose their shine. Sitting next to her is a man. He looks to be older than her, much older. He's well-dressed, as is she, in her red velvet gown with white lace and matching white gloves. An elegant hat adorns her head.

"Do you talk to her?" Valerie's voice is distant.

"No. She's only passing through town. We catch each other's eye, but…no."

"How do you feel?"

"Happy and sad at the same time."

"Why are you happy?"

"Because I saw her again and know she's alive and well."

"Why are you sad?"

"Because I know I won't see her again. Ever."

"Why don't you ever see her again?"

"She doesn't live here. She lives very far away and was just traveling through."

Isobel and Heather hold eye contact as the driver of the carriage climbs onto his seat, shakes the reins, and starts the horses moving. Isobel turns her head to watch as the carriage passes by her. She watches it leave, taking Heather away from her for the very last time.

Valerie's voice floated back. "I would like you to move now to the event and circumstances of your death in this lifetime. Remove yourself from any physical pain or discomfort, but note the events in the death experience. If you need to, you can take a step back and watch as it's happening from a safe distance. Know and remember what your thoughts and feeling are during this experience. One. Two. Three."

Delany took a deep breath and listened to Valerie's words from somewhere outside herself.

"Where are you?" Valerie asked.

"In the same cabin I was in when I was little and later came back to with Heather."

"What are you doing there?"

"I'm very sick. I'm in bed. There's a fire in the fireplace. Tomas is there with me."

"How old are you?"

"Forty-three."

"Did you ever get married?"

"No."

"It is going to be all right, Bellie," Tomas says, wiping Isobel's forehead with a cool cloth.

"Oh, Tomas," Isobel says. Her voice is weak as she struggles to talk. "It will not. But I am fine with that."

"That is the fever talking."

"It is not. I know it and you know it."

"You cannot leave me."

"You shall be fine. You have Kenna and that beautiful little girl of yours."

Tomas sits in a heavy wooden chair by his sister's side. He brushes the tears from his cheek as he watches her fade from this life into eternity.

Epilogue

That's the last of it." Delany set the heavy box down on top of another. "Abby said she'd be here with my sister and your mom around four to help us start unpacking." The last year with Jade had been wonderful. Delany couldn't wait to spend the rest of her life with her.

She warmed as Jade's arms slipped around her from behind. Jade rocked her gently from side to side and said, "That gives us almost three hours to christen our new home." She ran soft kisses up the side of Delany's neck.

Delany tilted her head to give Jade better access. "Only three hours? That's not enough time. There's so much I want to do with you and to you." She turned herself in Jade's arms until they were face-to-face.

Delany's pulse quickened as Jade's tongue entered her mouth. She closed her eyes and let herself be swept up in the feelings coursing through her body and settling squarely in her center. She would never tire of this woman's kisses. They were getting a second chance at love, and she was going to treasure every moment of it.

Jade pulled out of the kiss. "We don't have the bed set up yet and the couch is full of boxes. Where do you plan on having your way with me?"

"O ye of little faith." Delany located the large box marked

Open First and pulled at the tape sealing it shut. She drew out two jar candles wrapped in tissue paper and a box of wooden matches. She set the candles on the mantel of the stone fireplace. It was one of the features of the house that both she and Jade had fallen in love with. They'd put in their purchase offer within an hour of the real estate agent showing them the place.

With both candles lit, she returned to the box, pulled out a thick comforter, and laid it across the plush living room carpet. She emptied the box, extracting a bottle of wine, a corkscrew, two wineglasses, and a couple of pillows.

"Delany Payton, you never cease to amaze me." The smile on Jade's face was worth the effort.

Delany poured them each a glass of wine and handed one to Jade. Jade took two sips before setting the glass down on an end table and grabbing Delany by the shirt collar. Delany barely had time to put her glass next to Jade's before being pushed down onto the comforter with Jade on top of her.

What a wonderful way to start our new life together, Delany thought as Jade's hand slipped under her shirt. She silently blessed Isobel and Heather and the part of them that had continued on in her and Jade.

"I love you," Jade said.

"I love you, too. For now and all eternity."

About the Author

Creativity for Joy Argento (www.joyargento.com) started young. She was only five, growing up in Syracuse, New York, when she picked up a pencil and began drawing animals. These days she calls Rochester home, and oil paints are her medium of choice. Her award-winning art has found its way into homes around the globe.

Writing came later in life for Joy. Her love of lesbian romance inspired her to try her hand at writing, and she found her first self-published novels well received. She is thrilled to be a part of the Bold Strokes family and has enjoyed their books for years.

Joy has three grown children who are making their own way in the world and three grandsons who are the light of her life.

Books Available From Bold Strokes Books

All She Wants by Larkin Rose. Marci Jones and Tessa Dalton get more than they bargained for when their plans for a one-night stand turn into an opportunity for love. (978-1-63555-476-2)

Beautiful Accidents by Erin Zak. Stevie Adams doesn't believe in fate, not after losing her parents in a car crash. But she's about to discover that sometimes the best things in life happen purely by accident. (978-1-63555-497-7)

Before Now by Joy Argento. The instant Delaney Peyton and Jade Taylor meet, they sense a connection neither can explain. Can they overcome a betrayal that spans the centuries to reignite a love that can't be broken? (978-1-63555-525-7)

Breathe by Cari Hunter. Paramedic Jemima Pardon's chronic bad luck seems to be improving when she meets police officer Rosie Jones. But they face a battle to survive before they can find love. (978-1-63555-523-3)

Double-Crossed by Ali Vali. Hired thief and killer Reed Gable finds something in her scope that will change her life forever when she gets a contract to end casino accountant Brinley Myers's life. (978-1-63555-302-4)

False Horizons by CJ Birch. Jordan and Ash struggle with different views on the alien agenda and must find their way back to each other before they're swallowed up by a centuries-old war. Third in the New Horizons series. (978-1-63555-519-6)

Legacy by Charlotte Greene. In this paranormal mystery, five women hike to a remote cabin deep inside a national park—and unsettling events suggest that they should have stayed home. (978-1-63555-490-8)

Somewhere Along the Way by Kathleen Knowles. When Maxine Cooper moves to San Francisco during the summer of 1981, she learns that wherever you run, you cannot escape yourself. (978-1-63555-383-3)

Blood of the Pack by Jenny Frame. When Alpha of the Scottish pack Kenrick Wulver visits the Wolfgangs, she falls for Zaria Lupa, a wolf on the run. (978-1-63555-431-1)

Cause of Death by Sheri Lewis Wohl. Medical student Vi Akiak and K9 Search and Rescue officer Kate Renard must work together to find a killer before they end up the next targets. In the race for survival, they discover that love may be the biggest risk of all. (978-1-63555-441-0)

Chasing Sunset by Missouri Vaun. Hijinks and mishaps ensue as Iris and Finn set off on a road trip adventure, chasing the sunset, and falling in love along the way. (978-1-63555-454-0)

Double Down by MB Austin. When an unlikely friendship with Spanish pop star Erlea turns deeper, Celeste, in-house physician for the hotel hosting Erlea's show, has a choice to make—run or double down on love. (978-1-63555-423-6)

Party of Three by Sandy Lowe. Three friends are in for a wild night at billionaire heiress Eleanor McGregor's twenty-fifth birthday party. Love, lust, and doing the right thing, even when it hurts, turn the evening into one that will change their lives forever. (978-1-63555-246-1)

Sit. Stay. Love. by Karis Walsh. City girl Alana Brendt and country vet Tegan Evans both know they don't belong together. Only problem is, they're falling in love. (978-1-63555-439-7)

Where the Lies Hide by Renee Roman. As P.I. Camdyn Stark gets closer to solving the case, will her dark secrets and the lies she's buried jeopardize her future with the quietly beautiful Sarah Peters? (978-1-63555-371-0)

Beautiful Dreamer by Melissa Brayden. With love on the line, can Devyn Winters find it in her heart to stay in the small town of Dreamer's Bay, the one place she swore she'd never remain? (978-1-63555-305-5)

Create a Life to Love by Erin Zak. When sixteen-year-old Beth shows up at her birth mother's door, three lives will change forever. (978-1-63555-425-0)

Deadeye by Meredith Doench. Stranded while hunting the serial predator Deadeye, Special Agent Luce Hansen fights for survival while her lover, forensic pathologist Harper Bennett, hunts for clues to Hansen's disappearance along the killer's trail. (978-1-63555-253-9)

Endangered by Michelle Larkin. Shapeshifters Officer Aspen Wolfe and Dr. Tora Madigan fight their growing attraction as they work together to destroy a secret government agency that exterminates their kind. (978-1-63555-377-2)

Incognito by VK Powell. The only thing Evan Spears is focused on is capturing a fleeing murder suspect until wild card Frankie Strong is added to her team and causes chaos on and off the job. (978-1-63555-389-5)

Insult to Injury by Gun Brooke. After losing everything, Gail Owen withdraws to her old farmhouse and finds a destitute young woman, Romi Shepherd, living in a secret room. (978-1-63555-323-9)

Just One Moment by Dena Blake. If you were given the chance to have the love of your life back, could you ignore everything that went wrong and start over again? (978-1-63555-387-1)

Scene of the Crime by MJ Williamz. Cullen Mathew finds herself caught between the woman she thinks she loves but can no longer trust and a beautiful detective she can't stop thinking about who will stop at nothing to find the truth. (978-1-63555-405-2)

Fear of Falling by Georgia Beers. Singer Sophie James is ready to shake up her career, but her new manager, the gorgeous Dana Landon, has other ideas. (978-1-63555-443-4)

Daughter of No One by Sam Ledel. When their worlds are threatened, a princess and a village outcast must overcome their differences and embrace a budding attraction if they want to survive. (978-1-63555-427-4)

Playing with Fire by Lesley Davis. When Takira Lathan and Dante Groves meet at Takira's restaurant, love may find its way onto the menu. (978-1-63555-433-5)

Practice Makes Perfect by Carsen Taite. Meet law school friends Campbell, Abby, and Grace, law partners at Austin's premier boutique legal firm for young, hip entrepreneurs. Legal Affairs: one law firm, three best friends, three chances to fall in love. (978-1-63555-357-4)

The Last Seduction by Ronica Black. When you allow true love to elude you once and you desperately regret it, are you brave enough to grab it when it comes around again? (978-1-63555-211-9)

Wavering Convictions by Erin Dutton. After a traumatic event, Maggie has vowed to regain her strength and independence. So how can Ally be both the woman who makes her feel safe and a constant reminder of the person who took her security away? (978-1-63555-403-8)

A Bird of Sorrow by Shea Godfrey. As Darrius and her lover, Princess Jessa, gather their strength for the coming war, a mysterious spell will reveal the truth of an ancient love. (978-1-63555-009-2)

All the Worlds Between Us by Morgan Lee Miller. High school senior Quinn Hughes discovers that a broken friendship is actually a door propped open for an unexpected romance. (978-1-63555-457-1)

Falling by Kris Bryant. Falling in love isn't part of the plan, but will Shaylie Beck put her heart first and stick around, or tell the damaging truth? (978-1-63555-373-4)

An Intimate Deception by CJ Birch. Flynn County Sheriff Elle Ashley has spent her adult life atoning for her wild youth, but when she finds her ex, Jessie, murdered two weeks before the small town's biggest social event, she comes face-to-face with her past and all her well-kept secrets. (978-1-63555-417-5)

Cash and the Sorority Girl by Ashley Bartlett. Cash Braddock doesn't want to deal with morality, drugs, or people. Unfortunately, she's going to have to. (978-1-63555-310-9)

Secrets in a Small Town by Nicole Stiling. Deputy Chief Mackenzie Blake has one mission: find the person harassing Savannah Castillo and her daughter before they cause real harm. (978-1-63555-436-6)

www.ingramcontent.com/pod-product-compliance
Lightning Source LLC
Chambersburg PA
CBHW030513020726
47494CB00004B/1074